THE ICE PRINCESS

EMMY MORGAN

THE ICE PRINCESS

iUniverse books may be ordered through booksellers or by contacting:

iUniverse
1663 Liberty Drive
Bloomington, IN 47403
www.iuniverse.com
1-800-Authors (1-800-288-4677)

ISBN: 978-1-5320-6174-5 (sc)
ISBN: 978-1-5320-6173-8 (e)

Library of Congress Control Number: 2018914253

Print information available on the last page.

iUniverse rev. date: 11/29/2018

DEDICATION

To Grammy, Grampy, Brenda, Dan, Jamie, Dietrich, Nina, Mandee, Joe, Averi, Tyler, Macey, Nick, Ashley, Dominick, and the Kerrs, I love you so much for supporting me throughout the years; you've made me who I am today. They say you can't pick and choose your blood family; although this statement is true, I believe you can pick and choose what relationships you want to nurture and have endure.

To my friends I've grown up with, my coworkers I've stayed in touch with over the years, and the friends I made while living in Boston area, you've shown me the true meaning of the word friendship! And you're all going to Heaven for putting up with me. Shout out to Matt H.., Becky L., Alice F., Brandon D., Megan P., Melissa M., and all my friends that encouraged me to write this book and gave me guidance along the way.

Lastly to my Dream Team: Grandpa Sam, Grandma Ida, Lavalle, Kim, Omario, Graco, Grandma Vi, Ed, Heather, and Brett, thank you for watching over me. I want to thank you for not giving me everything I want, but for providing me with everything I need. I know I ask for a lot and boo hoo when things don't go my way, but somehow my Dream Team keeps me on the straight and narrow. Knowing you are all watching over me and pleading my case to "The Big Man," I know I will always be okay.

A special thank you to my aunt Emily. You let me be me. I wish I kept that necklace you gave me. "Unique" perfectly describes me.

"Don't cry because it's over, smile because it happened." Dr. Seuss

ACKNOWLEDGEMENTS

December 1992 during winter break I was watching "The Joan Rivers Show" on TV, and Joan had on a transsexual woman named Tula. Tula was a former "Bond Girl" and very active in the show business at the time; I thought she was absolutely beautiful. Tula was the first transgendered person I had ever encountered, and the first time I heard the term. The seed of an idea was planted in my head.

Late night months later, I was watching a British film called "Different for Girls" about a transgendered woman who ends up dating a guy she went to high school with. The idea of transsexuality again came into my head, and I quickly realized I had no idea what a transsexual was. The idea of a transgender love story started to circulate in my brain. I kept thinking about it over and over, but couldn't find any literature where a story like that was developed. That's when I decided to make my own book with a transgendered heroine.

A NOTE FROM THE AUTHOR

Thank you all for purchasing my book. For a long time I had no idea why I wrote this book, until January 26, 2015. I made the decision to fulfill a lifelong dream and transition from male-to-female on December 1, 2014, but it wasn't until my conversation with a Behavioral Specialist named Renee that we came to the conclusion together that this book is a manifesto of my feelings for my own future. Will I ever find love? When I do will he be the only one vying for my affections? If he isn't whom will I choose? How will my family, friends, and coworkers react?

Life imitated art because my family, friends, and coworkers all support me one-hundred percent (#3for3). I am so grateful to the people in my life; and I am even more grateful to be transitioning at this time in the world. No we aren't a perfect place to live, but it's been pretty damn close. Thank you for allowing me to be my authentic self.

PROLOGUE

As I stand with my eyes closed on the darkened stage at the Radio City Music Hall in New York City, I reflect on how far I've come in my life. The crowd applauds when my name is called.

"Ladies and gentleman." The overhead announcer says. "Please give your warmest of applause to tonight's Outstanding Supporting Actress first-time nominee Desiré Andersen. And last year's winner for Outstanding Younger Actor and nominee tonight please welcome Tom Pelphrey."

The lights go up onstage revealing me dressed in a custom made Atelier Versace gown. I am so nervous I don't extend my hand to Tom. He does, and I realize my cue. My sweaty palm grips his, and he winks. One of those "Just do like we rehearsed, and you'll be fine" winks.

Looking out at the crowd as we deliver our lines, I catch a glimpse of someone walking up the aisle towards the door. In the sea of people I recognize "that walk." The person's head turns, and I see his eyes. For a split second I forget where I am and that a billion people all over the world are watching me. I quickly recover with my punchline.

"Yeah, but will he make Mr. Blackwell's Best Dressed list?" I ask Tom. "Um I don't think so." The crowd laughs.

Tom fires back. "Whatever." He puts his fingers in the shape of a W.

Moments after announcing Ellen Degeneres the winner of Outstanding Talk Show, I am seated in the front row next to Joseph.

"Please welcome to the stage last year's winner for Outstanding Supporting Actor Greg Rikaart."

As the announcer summons Greg and he ascends the stage, I look over at Joseph; I'm completely ignoring Greg and his presence in front of me.

How did I get so lucky? I think to myself. *Statistics say as a Black transwoman I should be homeless, working in the sex industry, disowned by my family, no friends to speak on my behalf, beat up, raped, or murdered. Well I guess some of those things are true.* I pull back from Joseph and stare into his eyes.

"And the winner of the Daytime Emmy Award for Outstanding Supporting Actress is...Desiré Andersen." Greg exclaims.

The crowd erupts. Joseph turning to me clapping is the only thing that breaks my trance. I can see his lips moving, but the applause is too loud. He grabs my hands and stands me up bringing me in closer to him.

"You did it, baby." He shouts in my ear. "We made history."

My eyes widen at him as I now realize what he means. I throw my arms around his neck and cry. As I do I can see my life flash before me.

CHAPTER 1

I remember being six years-old playing with the tie of my black suit in the front row of the Springfield Funeral Parlor; while my mother stumbles towards the open casket. The black veil from her black pillbox hat barely conceals the mascara streaks on her dark brown face. One of her black gloved hands is firmly planted over the chest of her black dress suit; the other locked around my brother. Taking the jacket off of his black suit, Dorian tries his best to hold our mother up as she walks closer to the casket. Staring at her husband peacefully resting in the casket, she sobs uncontrollably. I walk up to comfort her, but Dorian pushes me back; defeated, I plop back into my seat swinging my legs back and forth under the seat. Mother throws herself onto the casket. Dorian and a few attendants peel her off it. Grandma Savannah motions for me; I rush over and sit with her. She hugs my shoulders.

I stood with a confused look on my face. *Why's mommy upset?* I thought to myself. *And why's daddy in that weird bed?*

Four years later ten year-old me sits in the front seat of the packed Ford Station Wagon as it turns on the road leading into Pheasant Hill Village in Feeding Hills (located south of Springfield, MA near the Connecticut border). Sixteen year-old Dorian is in the back seat listening to his Walkman with his earphones on while our mother drives.

"Wow, Mommy, this place looks beautiful," I exclaimed. Just then Dorian kicks under my seat. "Mommy, Dorian kicked my seat."

"Dorian, stop kicking the seat!" my mom says while looking into the rear view mirror.

Dorian innocently retorts, "I didn't. He's making it up. Remember how he made up that other story."

My mother pulls the car over onto the side of Pheasant Run Drive. She looks disapprovingly at me. "What did I tell you about making things up?"

"No, but he's fibbing. I don't fib." I protest.

Our mother sighs before finally putting the Station Wagon in "Park." She grips the wheel. "Now, we are in a new town. We are away from all that bad energy we had to endure since your father died. Do you think he'd want you acting up like this? Think about that."

I stare at my mother and can read in her eyes that I'm not her favorite child. "I'm sorry" is the only thing I could muster. I turn away and look out the window. This isn't gonna be as fun as I thought.

My mother smiles at me as she rubs the top of my head. She looks in the rear view mirror at Dorian's smirk. She again sighs to herself. If Dorian gets this behavior out now, maybe he won't feel the need to express himself later. He's a good kid just acting out because of his father's passing, she thinks to herself.

She manages a smile back at me as she looks up at the townhouse door to 36 Pheasant Run Drive. "I have so much hope that these kids get along." she whispers low enough for me to hear almost like she's talking to herself. She turns fully around and looks at Dorian whose smirk changes to a smile before turning back around. "I remember how helpful Dorian was when Kendrick and I brought Elijah home as a baby. Elijah's first few years of life were spent with Dorian's constant hovering over him. It wasn't until Elijah turned five Dorian's utter distain for Elijah's existence began to show. I can't seem to figure out why or what it was that changed."

Dorian, still shaking his head to the music from his Walkman, looks out the car window; he sees nothing. He rolls his eyes. The thought of now having to share a bedroom with someone I hate, someone I wish were never born, but also someone I will make miserable the entire time we are here. He smiles at the last thought as he turns the volume up on his Walkman.

And then it happened. Eight year-old Alicia saunters up with her siblings: six year-old triplets Bryant, Monica, and Rachel. The blond hair freckle- faced foursome stand at the passenger's side window. They wave and smile at me. I smile back and turn to my mother. She nods as I open the car door. The adorable blond foursome back up to give me room to get out.

CHAPTER 2

Northwest of Feeding Hills, MA in Northampton, twenty year-old me is backstage at The Grotto applying white eye shadow to my lids when my Razr rings. I throw my eye shadow brush down and tuck my straight black wig behind my right ear.

I flip open the cell phone as I pull up my white robe so my black heel doesn't get caught. I manage to make it to a corner of the room without falling. "Hello? Yeah, I'm out at a club." As I continue to listen to the caller on the other end, I cry and close the phone shut.

Jerome enters the back room primping his black curly wig dressed in a hot pink sleeveless button down tied at the waist black hot pants talking to Curtis. Curtis runs his fingers through his long black stringy wig; he is dressed identical to Jerome.

Curtis starts talking to Jerome in his native Spanish language; Jerome responds, "I'm Black not Hispanic."

With his thick Mexican accent Curtis replies, "Papi, I'm trying to learn you."

Jerome stops walking. "Explain to me how the hell you have such a thick Mexican accent when you were born and raised in Hartford, Connecticut NOT Mexico?" They both stop laughing noticing me crying in the corner.

They rush over to me. Through my tears I manage to mutter, "My grandma died tonight."

Curtis stares at me in disbelief. "The cute old lady from last week? Oh my god, Elijah, I'm sorry." He hugs then rocks me. "If you need to cancel tonight, Curtis and I will understand."

I free myself from his hug and compose myself as Curtis rubs my back. "No she would want the show to go on. Thank you, Jer." I hug Jerome before dapping my tears with a tissue in the mirror.

I finish applying the remainder of my makeup, disrobe revealing an identical outfit to both Jerome and Curtis, and comb my wig with my fingers.

As the lights go up onstage, I look out at the front table and see my grandmother's image smiling at me. When I blow a kiss in her direction the image disappears and is replaced by a group of exuberant gay men. The first beat of "Can't Get You Out of My Head" by Kylie Minogue begins.

When the last beat of the song finishes, the lights go down. Jerome and Curtis rush to collect the tips littering onstage as I rush backstage and burst back into tears.

Inside the Springfield Funeral Parlor, I sit once again in the front row.

Emotionally broken, I take the navy plaid handkerchief from the pocket of my navy pinstriped suit. Meanwhile my mother and Dorian sit somber one row behind me. Just as I am about to get up to the podium Dorian grabs my shoulder; I defiantly shrug Dorian off.

I muster up the strength to speak. "She was more than a grandmother. She was there for me..." Pausing, he stares at Dorothea and Dorian then continues. "as a mother and brother when others couldn't be. She was my best friend. She was my everything." I turn to the casket. "I love you, Gram. Selfishly I wish you were here, but if you're gone it means you are no longer doing painful chemo treatments and suffering every night. I can be happy you're not suffering now. I love you so much and will do everything in my life to make you proud."

I finally break down and a now eighteen year-old Alicia rushes over to me. She helps walk me past my mother and Dorian to sit with the now sixteen year-old triplets Bryant, Monica, and Rachel along with their parents, Ritchard and Kimberly.

As I look up through my tears to see Alicia, Bryant, Monica, Rachel, and Ritchard, I slowly close my eyes. In those few seconds the years of birthday parties, high school graduation parties, wedding anniversaries, 4th of July barbeques, Memorial Day weekend camping trips, Thanksgiving dinners, and Christmas mornings I spent with them that preceded that day flash by. When I open my eyes and turn to my mother and Dorian, images of the years of physical abuse at Dorian's hands, the incessant yelling my mother bestowed upon me, and the time I held a knife to Dorian's throat when I finally couldn't take any more of his abuse cycle one by one in my view. I will never forget the first time I saw real terror in Dorian's eyes or the smile I got upon seeing it. But that day in the funeral parlor I stand up with Alicia by my side to leave; Bryant, Monica, Rachel, and Ritchard follow us out.

Kimberly walks up to my mother who's standing near the casket. "Hi, Dorothea." She says touching my mother's shoulder. "Don't worry we'll take care of him."

My mother cocks her head back in defense. "I can only imagine what you think of me. After all these years, I'm really not a bad mother."

Kimberly removes her hand from my mother's forearm. "No, that came out wrong. Please I didn't mean it like that. I just meant..." but the hole had been dug. Kimberly feels herself blushing. Nervously she tucks her blond hair behind her left ear and uncomfortably smiles.

"No it's fine. Really." My mother says holding Dorian's arm. Dorian escorts my mother away giving Kimberly a "That-bitch-stands-in-judgment-of-me" look.

Later that night my mother flings open my bedroom door at our Pheasant Hill Village apartment. She scans the generic bedroom of twenty year old me illuminated by the moonlight from the blinds. Further in the room she scans over my high school diploma framed on my wall. She runs her fingers over my Structure badge lying on my nightstand. Opening my closet doors, she browses all my Structure men's clothing, both business and casual. She closes the doors, turns to leave, but notices a wooden handle sticking out from under my black metal futon. She kneels down, pulls it out, and plops it on my futon. She hesitates before opening it. She gasps seeing my short and long wigs, long and short sparkly performance dresses, and overstuffed makeup bag; she cups her mouth with both her hands trying to stifle her cries.

"This is what it feels like when teens give their children up for adoption." She whispers to herself while staring at the suitcase's contents uncupping her mouth. "Only mine is grown. He is going to hate me for the rest of his life, but I know this is the right thing to do. I have been such a bad mother to him. Kendrick, I know you are looking down disappointed in me. I'm sorry. I really am. But how can I do wrong by Dorian. He's your mini-me. I have to protect him. Elijah, we both knew, would be fine. We knew he was independent." She chuckles. "Remember after he was born, you said the other babies were all crying in the nursery till he came in. Wait, what did you say? He gurgled, "Hey quit that crying. You got nothing to cry about. We about to start our lives." She laughs through her tears. I let you down. I let him down, and now the best thing I can do is let him go. Don't hate me, please.

The sound of the front door opening and closing startles her. She scrambles to repack the suitcase and place it back to its original state under the bed. She stops just as she grabs the handle and reopens the suitcase. She wipes her tears and puts on the face of disapproval. The façade cracks for a second as she hears the footsteps coming up the stairs before forming back into place. When I open my bedroom door, to my surprise and shock my mother turns on the lamp resting on my nightstand.

CHAPTER 3

Two months later I sit at a conference table with Ritchard, Dorothea, Dorian, and my mother's sisters Priscilla Cole & Millicent Jackson in an office with a door tagged, Law Offices of Douglas & Douglas.

Reginald Douglas sits at the head of the cherry oak table sharply dressed in a white shirt and crazy pink tie with his sport coat on the back of his brown leather chair staring pensively at the document before him. I couldn't help but notice his almost graceful features.

As I look around the table I sit in silence. *The Last Will & Testament of my grandmother Savannah Phalba Baker. She had two daughters that didn't even show up at her damn funeral, another that mistreats her child, and a grandson she loves more than all of them. Well this won't go well at all I can predict.* I look over and Reginald is smoothing his curly dark brown hair back and adjusting his tie. *I need to find a way to unglue myself from these emotionally strapped, financially exhausted people who will definitely try contesting this will if it doesn't go in their favor. I just know they will. Especially my mother. Oh she will not like what's about to happen at all. Grandma didn't think too well of her.*

Reginald clearing his throat snaps me out of my own thoughts. "Shall we get started?" He asks but it comes out as a statement. Auntie Prissy, Aunt Millie, and my mother sit with Dorian on one side of the table while I and Ritchard sit on the other side.

Feels like battle lines drawn in the sand. This is how divorce cases must go I would imagine. I thought.

Reginald puts on the glasses he grabs from his shirt pocket and begins to read, "I Savannah Phalba Baker on Saturday, January sixth, nineteen ninety-six, being of sound mind and body hereby bequeath the following: To my first born daughter Priscilla Cole. You shall receive the title to my Cadillac which is fully paid for. You will have to put it in your name and get insurance for which I have left all access to my checking and savings accounts which total in excess of ten thousand dollars. I want to thank you for taking care of me when I needed you to. To my second daughter Millicent Jackson, I am leaving ownership of my homes in Centreville, Mississippi and Springfield, Massachusetts. We haven't seen eye to eye a lot of our lives, but you are still my child. I don't want you to ever worry about being homeless or evicted ever again. The houses are fully paid for the only things outstanding are the annual taxes which I have left you stocks and bonds to cover all costs. I, myself, inherited those stocks and bonds from my late husband and your father Emmanuel.

I would prefer you live in the Springfield home and use the Mississippi home as a family reunion slash vacation spot for our entire family. That home needs to stay with us as it truly is our family heirloom. To my youngest daughter Dorothea I leave my rare stamp and coin collections. I know it's not what you wanted, but you and Dorian have all you need; you two have always asked too much and given too little. I know Priscilla and Millicent probably were too emotionally distraught to attend my funeral; I understand as they didn't attend their daddy's for the same reason. But you Dorothea, you always show up when you need something and you raised Dorian to be the same way. Not that you will but I hope you learn from this and heed my words: I did not raise you to be a selfish, spoiled brat. Maybe that is your daddy's fault, but the way you favor Dorian over Elijah is disgusting. Whatever your reasons are your child is your child is your child. I do not have a favorite. I love you baby girl, but I don't much like you. With all that being said the only one left is my beloved grandson, Elijah. Before you say anything Prissy and Millie, I have already given your kids what I needed to give them privately. Elijah is special, so don't any of you go blaming him for anything. Elijah Davis, my beautiful, brave boy I leave you a trust fund your late grandfather and I have set up with you as the beneficiary worth $1,000,000; the stipulations of the trust fund include an automatic monthly payout of $5,000 into your bank account, but will allow you to withdraw a large amount only to purchase a home or automobile, for educational or work-related purposes, and/or for medical or funeral expenses. Your friend Ritchard Andersen will be the sole trustee of this trust fund. Ritchard, please make sure you and your wife take care of my baby boy. You and I have had long talks recently so I know you will." Reginald looks up from reading to see me smiling. "That's it for family." Reginald says. "The rest are cousins and friends whom I can't read to you." Priscilla & Millicent walk over to me and give me a long-overdue hug. Dorian & Dorothea stand up and leave without saying a word to anyone. Ritchard walks over to Reginald.

As Priscilla & Millicent walk out of the office down the hall ignoring Kimberly sitting on a bench against the opposite wall of the Conference Room; she stands up when Ritchard and I walk out behind my aunts. Kimberly picks a piece of lint from Ritchard's sandy blond hair. He grabs her hand and kisses it. As the three of us board the elevator, Dorothea and Dorian walk up behind us. Inside the elevator Kimberly, Ritchard, and I turn around just as the elevator doors close in front of Dorothea and Dorian on the other side. I turn to Ritchard & Kimberly as he releases his finger from the "Close Doors" button.

Sitting at one end of the Andersen dining room table, I pause while talking to Alicia, Bryant, Monica, Rachel, Ritchard, and Kimberly.

How do I even explain this? I think. "You know how you don't want to be a woman?" I direct at Bryant who nods. "Well it's the opposite for me. It's something I've thought about my entire life, but I guess I never thought I could do it. With my Gram's money I can now."

"Yeah but will you grow huge boobs?" Bryant asks but I ignore his question.

"I wanna see it when you're done." Monica states.

"NO! It's called privates for a reason." I reply in disgust.

"Oh come on." Alicia chimes in. "It's not every day you see a man-made vagina. It's gonna be cool. Don't you wanna show it off?"

"NO!" I exclaim as I turn my head to laugh.

After the conversation they each hug me. Kimberly walks me to the front door. As soon as the door closes behind me Ritchard rushes over to the oak computer desk with everyone gathered around him. Kimberly breaks from the group and dials a number on the cordless phone. On the other end my mother sees the number and walks away; Kimberly replaces the cordless in its charger without leaving a message. Monica walks over to the printer and grabs <u>Harry Benjamin's Transgender Standards of Care</u> that Ritchard printed out.

I lie back on a black quilted chaise lounge in Dr. Guinta's office. I talk as the be speckled woman seated next to me writes on her notepad and nods. I tell this paid stranger everything from my childhood and how I always longed to be a woman to being an adult and never quite feeling an attraction to gay men but moreso to straight men. The good doc and I realize it has to stem from birth. My brother and I both grew up with a mom and dad, but I loved dressing up in my mother's clothing, putting on her makeup and her Wingsong perfume. So why me and not him? These weekly sessions continue for a year. I learn more about myself and how I was pretty much diagnosed by my friend Alicia when we were kids. Lil spitfire that she was. Of course neither of us knew what transgender was, but she knew before I did that I was born in the wrong body.

Inside my newly decorated apartment Alicia gingerly applies makeup to my face in front of my bedroom mirror with my blinds open to get maximum natural light. She talks to me about something called contouring. Monica and Rachel sit on my bed hanging off of every word Alicia says taking mental notes. Done with my makeup, Alicia walks me over to the different work outfits she has laid on my bed behind Monica and Rachel. I put up one finger to them signaling them to "hold on a minute," and rush into my bathroom shutting the door behind me.

I grab my daily Estrogen shot, inject it in my arm, place the used needle in the trash, and exit the bathroom. As I wedge my feet into the tiny heels, Alicia demonstrates how to properly shave my legs with broad strokes upward. Monica and Rachel are still enthralled as Bryant peaks in from the living room. Fully dressed as a woman, I saunter into the living room. Monica and Rachel following me. Bryant is taken aback at first but then looks me from toe to head.

Bryant's face creates a smile. "You look beautiful." He hugs me; Bryant looks past me at Monica, and Rachel. He spies Alicia still in my bedroom touching up the makeup on her shoulder covering up a bruise.

I walk over to the long mirror in my hallway to see my full profile. *The dark brown wavy wig fits perfectly on my head falls just at his shoulders.* I say to myself. *The brown Victoria's Secret lace tank shows just enough cleavage.* I adjust to tuck in the breast form that popped out of the side. I run my hand down the light blue Diesel jeans. Looking down at my feet, I wiggle my purple pedicured toes in my glitter leather strappy Jimmy Choo sandals. *I do look beautiful.*

CHAPTER 4

nd so begins my journey. First up coming up with a name. Staring at myself in the mirror I can only think of one name that fits: Desiré.
Wait Desiré Davis? Yuck. I scrunch my face at the sound of that name in my head. *No wait what about Desiré Andersen. Yes. Perfect.* I smile. *Wait I'm gonna need a middle name. Hmm Desiré Savannah Andersen? No that's too long. Desiré Kimberly-no.* It comes to me like a slap in the face. *Taylor.* My eyes begin to fill with tears of a friend long since passed. $165 dollars later on my legally binding Certificate of Name Change, social security card, Massachusetts driver's license (with a Glamour Shots new photo), health insurance and dental cards, Big Y and Stop N Shop rewards cards, American Express Platinum card, AAA card, car registration, Bank of America checking, savings, and debit card. It took all of two days to change my name as beneficiary on my trust fund; I think that was more to do with Ritchard being a bulldog to get me my money than the world being so progressive.

Dr. Rosario said I will be on Estrogen shots for the rest of my life in order to replace the testosterone in my body. Had I transitioned when I was younger things like my voice and breast development would've happened earlier on. Now that I'm older my vocal chords have already formed so my voice won't change. My breasts... looks like I'm what I always wanted to be: a teenage girl. I'm starting from puberty. Dr. Rosario said the first three years will be my puberty and my breasts will grow in the most then. Typically, she said, most girls are a cup size smaller than their mothers. *Great I'm gonna have C's. I want full B's.* I stand up shirtless with my wig on and look at my flat chest in my bedroom mirror. *I don't have the frame for C's. They'll look like bowling balls on my chest. UGH*

During those first six months is when my life changed the most.

I came out as transgender to my boss at Structure, Lynnette. I know, I know. I have a monthly stipend from my trust fund. I do not need to work. But I've been working here part-time all through college and now after. I couldn't leave this job. It's been like a second home. And Lynnette has always been there for me although she'll be the first to admit she's only ever had gay friends, but has never had any experience with a transsexual (back then people called us transsexuals whether we were transmen or transwomen. I hate that term, and tranny is the transworld's form of the N word for Black folk. I had to educate Lynnette that I was a transwoman meaning I was transitioning into a woman. A transman transitions into a man hence the terms). For the first I'd say four or five months she kept calling me Elijah and referring to me as he or him. I didn't get mad. Hey, it showed me I didn't change whom I am inside to her. To her I was still her part-time employee. It was nice to hear a customer call me "Miss" though. At first I didn't realize he was talking to me as I folded clothes behind the cash wrap. When I finally realized I acknowledged him with a smile.

My other "womanly" moment came as I was walking up the escalators in the mall; they are always broken. I felt my boobs bounce on my chest. I looked down thinking something must've fallen on them and realized I had grown full A cups. When I got home I also realized the continual months of itching meant they were growing. And the bruises underneath my boobs were because my ever growing boobs were pushing the gel forms down on the padding of my lace Victoria's Secret bras. It took three weeks for the bruising to subside.

I'd always had a thin body growing up, but noticed my waist was more synched and my hips wider. I did a quick tape measure session in my bathroom standing in my bra and undies. *Five foot eight inches tall. Thirty-four inch breast. Thirty inch waist. Thirty-four inch hips. Wow if my waist was four inches smaller I could walk the catwalk alongside Cindy Crawford, Naomi Campbell, and Claudia Schiffer. WOW! Desiré Andersen. Supermodel.* I giggled as I threw on my leopard print robe and left my bathroom.

Another female epiphany occurred. I was walking into the mall running a touch late and someone held open the door for me. I didn't think anything of it especially when I held the door behind me for him. But then another time I was walking into the movie theaters from the parking lot and a group of guys were ahead of me. The group of three parted in the middle to let me past them, one grabbed the door for me, then as I realized there was a fourth in their party, that guy held open the second door for me to enter through. To them I was a young woman in my twenties; I wasn't a transwoman. I also noticed when I shopped at stores, especially Christmas shopping for Bryant at Strawberries, the nerdy but hot cashiers would talk to me and dare I say flirt. Oddly enough I was still a virgin. I guess you can say the past still haunted me. I wasn't in the space for dating.

The life I wanted to lead since I was a kid was here. I was a transwoman in the truest sense. And happier than I had ever been. I think to myself as I pee in a stall in the women's bathroom at G. Fox. *I hope no one is peeking into this stall because I am smiling like an idiot simply because I am peeing in the women's room.* I stand up, let the residual pee exit my body (I hate it so much now I don't even call it by name), wipe "it" clean of pee, pull up my panties along with my jeans, and start buttoning my jeans. As soon as I move a tiny bit forward the toilet flushes itself. I turn around startled. *Is some secret hand flushing my toilet?* That's when I notice the fancy new motion sensor. With that sigh of relief I continue buttoning, grab my cell phone from the top of the tampon disposal can, free my purse from the hook on the back of the stall door, and walk out. I put my cross body purse over my head and propped on my shoulder as to wash my hands. I notice the woman next to me fixing her hair then wiping the counter with a paper towel of her loose hairs and water. *Geesh women are clean. They really take care of their bathroom. Our bathroom. Whatever.* Finished washing my hands thoroughly the woman pulls down enough paper towel for me to dry my hands. I smile, and she smiles back before leaving. I decide to pull down enough paper towels for the next person and leave. *It's all about women helping each other.*

It's not all rainbows and sunshine though. I wish someone would've told me I have to shave my face, legs, stomach, chest, feet, butt crack, butt hole, and lower back. Sure hormones thin out the hairs but they are still growing. And when you have a... thing wearing women's jeans and skirts accentuate it. Thankfully there's no way to tell my boy jeans are actual boy jeans; I still wear them. And if I wanna wear any of the cute sandals I bought in the Old Navy clearance bin last month, I need to make sure I get a pedicure at least monthly. Of course that means I need to get my nails done. Great, now I have to find a place that won't freak out seeing a transwoman walk in; it was weird enough walking into Sally's Beauty Supply trying to find a wig. Wait, Alicia can do my nails; she's good at doing Monica & Rachel's. My favorite "wish someone woulda told me" is how my boobs are growing differently. One is fuller and less pointy than the other. I call them M&M though; they'll melt in your mouth not in your hand...HELLO!

It's funny to Ritchard, Kimberly, Alicia, Bryant, Monica, Rachel, Kimberly's parents Grampy and Grammy (legally William and Barbara, but they are my Grampy and Grammy), and the rest of Kimberly's family (Ritchard' was an only child with all his family in England), I was Desiré. At this point I had zero contact with "my Black family." Maybe Kimberly called my mother I don't know, but I hadn't spoken to Dorian, my mother, my aunts, my uncles, or my cousins in a while. They were no longer a priority for me. No it was all about "my White family." The Andersens were accepting, loving, and truth be told this had been coming for decades. There was nothing and no one that could tell me they were not my family. I was living with Ritchard & Kimberly after the incident with my mother. Ugh, Dorothea. I know biologically I'm tied so she'll always be my mother, but Kimberly was always and is my mom. She will be Dorothea from now on. But back to my point it was the Andersens who helped me find an apartment, the Andersens who helped me move into an apartment, the Andersens who I still spent those birthday parties, high school graduation parties, wedding anniversaries, 4th of July barbeques, Memorial Day weekend camping trips, Thanksgiving dinners, and Christmas mornings with. This was my new normal. To them I am a daughter, a sister, and a granddaughter.

CHAPTER 5

Fourteen months later I'm sitting at a desk next to Kimberly & Ritchard as we stare at a computer enhanced image of me with two saline breast implants across from Dr. Vigue, one of Boston's best plastic surgeons. I catch a glimpse of my curly bobbed naturally dark brown hair and much more feminine face.

Hormones are working just fine. I smile at myself as Dr. Vigue details the difference between saline and silicone breast implants.

After, I ultimately decide not to have breast augmentation my first of three surgeries.

First was a procedure where doctors pull and flatten the vocal chords to raise the pitch called Feminization Largynoplasty; a natural side effect is the Adam's apple shrinks. Dr. Harvey told me the dangers of me losing my voice completely or the voice being too high could be an end result. I didn't care. I wanted all traces of Elijah Davis off my body.

Weeks later in a hospital room I'm lying in a Johnnie and cap on a gurney while Kimberly kisses my hand, she rubs my arm as a slow drip releases. My eyelids begin to get heavier and heavier with every stroke on my arm. I slowly close my eyes as Ritchard leads Kimberly to the Waiting Area where Alicia, Bryant, Monica, and Rachel are sitting with Grampy and Grammy.

And the big one; the surgery that will officially make Elijah Davis physically Desiré Andersen. Dr. Grodecki goes over the actual Gender Reassignment Surgery called Vaginoplasty, where the vagina is formed from inverting the penis into the body creating a vagina cavity. Six or seven months later I would go back in for my Labiaplasty surgery which creates a more realistic labia. Of course my white family was there both in the doctors' offices during consultation and in the waiting rooms during the surgeries.

A few days after my Labiaplasty at my kitchen table, my bandaged body once again hunches over forms, this time to change my legal gender marker. That brief four hours sitting alone in my apartment I manage filling out my Massachusetts driver's license, Birth Certificate, and U.S. Passport. The cute Asian guy at the Social Security Office told me he changed my gender marker the day I came in to change my name on my social.

"Ms. Andersen, as far as the Federal Government is concerned you are a female" he said with the biggest smile ever. It's funny how some people say they aren't racist yet they aren't attracted to Asians. Anyone who ever said that would eat their words looking at this man. I so wanted to get Thomas' number. But I realized how completely inappropriate that'd be.

Kimberly wanted to have a "Becoming Desiré" party to reintroduce me to everyone as Desiré, but hours later as I sleep, Kimberly quietly tiptoes out of my bedroom with a tray of empty dishes. Bryant is holding open the door and shuts it softly behind Kimberly as Bryant slithers himself inside the bedroom. He lies in bed next to me; I roll over and puts my arm around his stomach. He kisses the top of my head and settles into sleep resting his head on mine. He crosses his feet while the TV displays an episode of *"Guiding Light."* Within minutes Bryant is fast asleep. Monica and Rachel sneak in, draw a penis with washable black marker on his forehead, and take a picture of him with their cell. They sneak out giggling.

Dressed in a mint green halter top jersey dress and hair in a tight bun at the base of my head, I fidget in front of Monica and Rachel both in identical gowns and hairstyles at the church altar. I tug up the white ribbon around my waist. Bryant stands in a black tux on the Groom's side behind Alicia's fiancé Damian Wilson in an identical tux. Damian wipes the sweat from his shiny pale white bald head. All the guests in the church stand as a veiled Alicia in her Vintage Givenchy white Lily of the Valley strapless wedding gown. With Ritchard escorting her by her arm she descends the aisle as the Bridal March plays.

Why is she going through with this? I ask myself. *She must be pregnant.*

At the altar I stare with worried eyes at Alicia. She must've felt it because she suddenly looks at me. As she does I smile, but that's when I see it. Peeking up from her back is a small bruise. Without even thinking I move forward to bring her dress up. She smiles at me.

"It looked like it was moving too far down." I whisper loudly in case anyone else noticed. Alicia's face registers shock.

The ceremony continues without a hitch; while I avoid direct conversation with Alicia. Instead I perform my mandatory duties as Maid of Honor like giving her bouquet back to her as the ceremony concludes, helping her turn in her dress, walking arm-in-arm with Damian's overly flirtatious cousin Lionel, and at the reception hall taking the microphone in one hand from the DJ and raising my glass of champagne in the other.

"Damian, you are a lucky man." I firmly state. "I hope in the years to come you get exactly what you deserve with respect to my best friend and sister, Alicia. I'm happy for you, little sis. And thank you for introducing me to your wonderful family. Here, here." Everyone claps after my speech. I'm summoned to pose for pictures with first the bridal party then the Andersen family. Kimberly's sister Deborah walks over on braces with her husband Kenneth helping her. I rush over and hug her then him. Their daughters Hayley and Olivia follow her and hug either side of me. The photographer snaps a picture of me with Hayley and Olivia, Alicia, Monica, & Rachel; then another with all of us and our childhood friends Connie Petersen and Leelee Baxter. My face hurt that night from the ear-to-ear smile I had all day.

CHAPTER 6

I waltz into the showroom at Mazda of Agawam and scan the room. My eyes are diverted to the "2003 Fall Clearance Sale" banner. They lower to lock on a grey 2004 Mazda hatchback parked in the center of the showroom. I once again scan, but this time at the cubicles littered around three sides of the hatchback and along the glass walls. In one cubicle a middle aged Asian couple sits with a middle aged Caucasian salesperson across from them mulling over paperwork. An older Hispanic man stands up next to a younger version of himself barking at a young nervous Caucasian salesperson. Two younger Caucasian saleswomen gossip near the hatchback in the center of the showroom, before an elderly Caucasian couple walk up to them.

With my newly installed 20/20 vision thanks to my contacts I can make out "Crasso Lozano" on the nametag of the olive skinned dark haired young salesperson approaching me.

"Hey I'm Crasso. Welcome to Mazda of Agawam. May I be of assistance to you?" Crasso robotically asks.

I talk to him like I'm a ditz; yup I plan on working him like a fiddle. I had just seen Marilyn Monroe in *"How to Marry A Millionaire"* so of course I began batting my eyes. He asked if I had something in my eye; guess that technique didn't work out so well. Or maybe it did. He wanted to sell me the base model sister of the car I really wanted. Somehow we ended up at the car in the middle of the showroom.

Being as close as I am to the car I can now see a cubicle with the nameplate "Sloane Williams" - under it Finance Manager. I realize I'm caught as my eyes move from the sign to greet Sloane's. He notices and reciprocates a smile.

Crasso and I move to his cubicle across from Sloane's and continue our chat. Crasso leaves for a minute before returning with Mazda keys. He tells me to wait outside, then his fellow employees open the showroom doors as he drives the show car out onto the sales lot in front of me. As Crasso opens the door to climb out of the Driver's side, I climb into his place. Fully buckled in we drive off.

We walk back into the showroom thirty minutes later. Crasso walks ahead of me with the keys.

"Happy you like the car, Desiré. I'll see what I can do," Crasso says as he replaces the keys in the car case.

"That'd be very nice of you." I say as I walk inside and sit at the chair in front of his desk. I smile as he disappears into Sloane's cubicle. A few minutes go by, and Crasso walks over smiling.

Sitting alone at Sloane's desk, I smile at Sloane who smiles back.

"Listen," I reason. "I want this car. The sticker stays 26, but I know that's a high ass mark-up. I will pay you 18 now via check." I grab my checkbook from my purse along with a pen. "Whom should I make this check out to?"

Stunned into silence Sloane stumbles on his words. "Well, Mazda of Agawam."

As I finish signing my name on the check, I extend it to him, then draw it back. "Actually what about 15?"

Enraged Sloane spits. "That's a 3,000 dollar drop. What the hell?"

I smile slyly. "A check over 10,000 dollars will take at least three days to clear, especially with it being Saturday. The bank won't even touch the first 5,000 till Monday. I do, in fact, have my debit card with me. We can get this purchase taken care of immediately."

Sloane stares at me strangely. At first I was okay, but soon I felt uncomfortable. "Well I know a way you can make up for that 3,000."

A date? Fine. I mean what's the worst that can happen? I think to myself as I smile.

When Crasso pops in to talk to Sloane briefly, I lean over with my debit card. "Here ya go. You can run that through if you wish. I'll be waiting." I lean back in my chair. Sloane takes my debit card and walks away with Crasso.

Ten minutes later, Sloane returns with my debit card, the unsigned sales receipt, a customer receipt, a pen, and more documents for me to sign. *Has any one person signed their name so many times before?* I begin signing away as he explains page by page all the documents. After the third document, I am simply signing my name tuning out whatever he's saying. I grin when Sloane stands up and hands me the keys.

Sloane smiled. "So about that extra 3?"

Later that evening I drive back to the dealership in my new Mazda. As I park a bad feeling sweeps over me. I brush it off.

"Why'd we have to do it here?" I ask while shutting the door and alarming the car.

"Because it's more private." He says as I enter back in the showroom looking around.

"What about in there?" Sloane motions towards the conference room off the right. "No, in here," he calls in the dark.

I look to my left now noticing he's gone. I navigate in the dark towards his voice ending up in his cubicle. He is outlined by the single overhead emergency light shining in the showroom. He leans against his desk with his butt on the desk ledge. I then realize walking towards him my dress hugs every curve of my body. *Am I inviting this wearing this?*

Before I know what's happening, Sloane pulls me into him as his lips engulf my mouth. His grip on me is so tight I feel him get excited...down there. Although his lips are soft I am so turned off.

I pull back and look at him. "I'm not a biological woman; I'm a transwoman." He immediately releases me.

Without responding to me, he again passionately kisses me while unbuckling his belt and shimmying his pants down his legs. It was all happening so fast yet in slow motion. I tried walking away but somehow in the dark his arms latched around me. His grip was like chains of steel. He flipped me around and held my wrists down against his desk.

"No. No." I said it very clear. But he either thought I meant yes or didn't care.

There on his desk in the sparsely lit cubicle, he reached under my dress with his free hand, ripped off my panties, pushed up the back of my dress, slapped my bare ass, and raped me. I cried, said "Ow," and cried some more. When I tried moving forward so would he. He thought I was trying to find his fuck rhythm. I was trying to get away. He leaned in and whispered in my ear. But his words were drowned out by "Alone." Someone forgot to turn the radio off, so Heart's hit song soared overhead as the soundtrack to this awful experience.

I should've just paid eighteen. I thought to myself as he finally climaxed inside of me.

He breathed heavily before falling on my back. The weight of him made me collapse on the desk. He stood up, leaned over, and grabbed a tissue from his desk. As he pulled out I pushed him back into a chair. I grabbed my torn panties on the floor, my keys on his desk, and ran. I think he was calling after me but I kept running. I was still inside the showroom when I unlocked my car remotely. I didn't want to waste time. I threw open the door and could now hear his footfalls behind me. I ran to my car, opened the door, slammed it shut, and put the key in the ignition. I looked up to see him just reaching the door when my car started. I turned the car over and peeled out. I flew into oncoming traffic on the main road next to the dealership. At the first red light down the street I put on my seatbelt. I was shaking and began to cry. Then I felt it. As I looked down I saw the pool of blood begin to form under my legs. The car behind me beeped. I shot my head forward and slammed on the accelerator.

Walking into my apartment slowly I knew I should be at the hospital. They say you shouldn't wash away medical evidence, but none of them had been raped. None of them had been violated the way I was violated. Like a zombie I moved through my apartment and managed to make my way to my bathroom. Just as I was about to turn on the water in my shower I thought about what would happen if I didn't go to the hospital right now. *What if Sloane was a serial rapist? Could I be his first or fourth victim?* Common sense and logic took over.

Unshowered and still in my rape clothing, I sat on a towel as I drove myself to Baystate Medical Center.

CHAPTER 7

Music pumps out of the speakers inside The Grotto. A rather buff Caucasian man dressed like a sexy Pilgrim takes money from the next patron in line; a tall African-American man dressed like a sexy Native American Chief holds a box labeled "2004 Thanksgiving Food Drive." A mixture of different raced men dressed as sexy Native Americans and sexy Pilgrims serve shots to clusters of people. Gay men gyrate on the dance floor to the music. Two Asian male Bartenders dressed as Wartime Soldiers work both sides of the bar. With my legs crossed, dressed as Pocahontas, I sit on a stool at the bar as Marcus Pagano approaches me.

"I'm Marcus." He screams leaning near my ear.

I turn around and laugh like he's said something funny. "Pretend like we know each other."

Marcus joins in my charade as a thickly mustached very thin man walks by. Marcus looks directly at the man.

"That's my stalker." I tell him while kissing Marcus on the cheek.

Stumbling into Marcus' cramped studio apartment, Marcus and I kiss while tearing off each other's clothes. He closes the front door with his foot. We reach the bed completely naked; he fumbles putting the condom on until I take the condom from him. I roll the condom on my finger, pop it in my open mouth, then kneel down in front of him placing the condom on his hard penis. I stand up, push him back onto the bed, and straddle him. His hands run over my body gripping my hips; together we move up and down. As he loudly climaxes, I start to cry. I bury my face in his chest as he finishes. He kisses my neck. *I bet he thinks these are tears of joy.*

As his hands run up and down my back as he kisses my forehead. "That was so fucking amazing."

"Really?" I lift my head up to look at him.

Marcus moves my hair to expose my neck. He tries kissing my lips. He stops short when he sees my tears. "Whoa. Those weren't tears of joy huh?"

"No sorry." I wipe my own tears away. "I dunno what I'm doing here. I…" *Should I tell this complete stranger? Well what the hell he just fucked me.* "I was raped. And when I went to the hospital the rape kit was processed, and they still couldn't find my rapist so I dunno I guess I thought maybe you could…I dunno. This is dumb." He stops me from leaving. He looks like he wants me to continue. "I thought we've been talking for a month or so maybe us having sex would…sorry this is dumb." He sweetly kisses my lips before anchoring me against his headboard. He pins himself on top of me and more passionately kisses me. He releases me to grab another condom from his nightstand drawer. I stay locked in place waiting for him. He takes off the used one and throws it in the nearby wastebasket, and puts on a new one before we start another round of animalistic love making.

Now fully dressed, I tiptoe out of his apartment carrying my brown gladiator shoes with my purse tucked under my arm. I quietly shut the front door behind me.

Inside my apartment I walk past my answering machine that's lit with 50 messages. Marcus' number starts blowing up my cell.

I turn on the TV and sit on my couch. The peace and quiet makes me face things.

"I am not happy." I say out loud to myself. "I did what I was supposed to do as a victim of rape and feel like because I am a transwoman no one is taking it serious." I stand up. "Almost like because I am a transwoman I deserved it or invited it." And now I get mad. "WELL FUCK YOU! HE RIPPED MY VIRGINITY AWAY FROM ME! I WILL NEVER HAVE THE CHANCE TO CHOOSE WHOM I WANTED TO BE THAT PERSON FOR ME!!!!!" I break down crying.

Crying because I can still feel him inside me. Crying because I know my attacker and cannot do anything about it. Crying because I left Marcus alone. Crying because I haven't talked to my white family in two months. Crying because I haven't cried like this since my grandma Savannah died.

I end up crying so hard and for so long I fall asleep on the couch wrapped in the blanket Monica made me last year for my birthday.

CHAPTER 8

In my living room I change the Alaye calendar from November 2004 to December 2004 above my computer at my desk. The knock at my front door sends me to my feet. Marcus walks in kissing my cheek. I close the door behind him.

"God I'm so glad you called. I missed you" He says as he hugs me.

I smile. "Me too. I'm sorry about what happened before, but hey a lot has happened since we last hung out." Marcus nods as he sits on the couch anxious to hear. "Well…" I sit next to him. He leans over and kisses my neck. "I decided to go full-time at Structure; I start Monday. Tomorrow I have lunch with my white parents. And I'm sorry."

"Listen, I don't know about all this." He pulls back.

I pull my head back in confusion. "All what?"

"Don't wig out, but I just mean us. This. You're hot and all and I love having sex with you, but I'm not really looking for a relationship." He grabs my wrist as I'm about to stand up, but I manage to push him away. "Give me a fucking break." He sits back into the couch pillows. "I'm straight okay. This is tough okay. My family wouldn't be okay with-"

"It's even tougher being a fucking man and taking responsibility for your decisions." I confidently say to him. I fold my arms across my chest standing up looking down on him. *Come back with something. I dare you.* I think to myself.

"Are you fucking serious?" He shoots up to his feet. "YOU lecturing ME on being a man?" He laughs. "Please tell me you're joking."

"You know what?" I move to the front door and open it. "You need to leave."

"We aren't done talking." He closes it with one hand.

I pull at the knob trying to open the door, but his strength keeps it closed. "Yes we are." I say still struggling to open the door. "Get the fuck out."

"No we aren't." He pushes me back, and I land on the couch. "Stay right fucking there." He points at me.

"FUCK YOU." I scream grabbing my cordless phone on the end table. "Get the fuck out, or I will call the cops." His face changes to Sloane's. *I was raped once; I won't let it happen again.* I stand with the phone in my hand as a weapon. I am ready to beat the shit out him till he's dead with that phone.

I turn away from him to dial, but he rushes over and grabs the phone from me with one hand; he backhands me with the other. I fall against the couch again but this time holding my face.

He drops the phone in what I can only register as shock and rushes over to me. "Oh my god. I'm sorry."

I take this as my cue to release all my rage and anger. I lunge at him landing on his chest, he falls back on the ground, I pull his hair, spit on him, and start punching him wildly all while screaming "I HATE YOUR FUCKING GUTS! GET OUT OF MY HOUSE YOU SICK FUCK!" I can feel him trying to wiggle out from under me. Even with him being a good hundred pounds heavier my adrenaline and anger pins him down. I'm still screaming every curse word I can think of while hitting him and scratching at him. I'm trying to find some way to make him bleed, when he finally kicks me off. Square in the gut. The shock of being kicked forces me out of my rage episode. He scrambles to his feet and runs towards the door without saying one word. Still in shock the force of his kick makes me gasp for air. By that time he's unlocked the door and ran out. I lie on the floor for a few minutes trying to catch my breath before getting up and closing the door.

CHAPTER 9

My naturally dark brown hair has grown out just below my shoulders. I dub tonight "Wigless Wednesday" as I walk into the Hippodrome. Feeling confident in my light brown lace sleeveless top and skinny jeans I scan the club standing on my tiptoes to look above the stares from the crowd.

Typical Springfield crowd of overdressed women and underdressed men. The women look like they all shop at Forever 21's Bargain bin, and the men wear clothes that were nice back in 1998 when Metrosexual was a word people used freely.

Trying not to stare directly into anyone's eyes I walk up a small flight of stairs into the club under a banner reading "2005 Day after New Year's." I roll my eyes at the monotony of the room. Directly in front of me is the bar packed on all four sides with patrons demanding service. As I turn my head to walk further into the club, I'm momentarily blinded by one of the green laser beams rotating from the ceiling around the room. It's joined by its red and yellow counterparts affixed from the ceiling. The couple arguing loudly to my left force me to turn to look in their direction. A group of girls stumble drunk past me; one is wearing a "Bride" tiara.

After almost three minutes of scanning the room I find Alicia. I clutch my Coach wristlet closer to my body as I move through the crowd. I sneak up behind Alicia to purposely startle her; we hug when she turns around. I then hug Connie & Leelee whom are standing close by. Connie is a medium height thin Asian girl; in contrast to Leelee who's a shorter slightly curvy blond Caucasian girl. Both are dressed in almost identical knee length peasant dresses except Connie's has a blue paisley pattern with no waist, and Leelee's is red accentuated with a gold belt. Behind the girls with their back to me stand two tall muscular Caucasian men with matching dark brown hair. Even from the back if you picked up the latest issue of <u>Abercrombie & Fitch Quarterly</u> they would've been in there. As they turn around my heart fell to my feet. I could feel my face about to drop, but I picked it back up.

Pretend you don't know them. My brain tells my heart.

I decide to ignore the younger one with slightly longer hair; his older counterpart has a short Caesar cut that I give a slight smirk to. I instinctively grab Alicia by the hand who grabs Leelee's hand who grabs Connie's hand as they walk to the dance floor. The two guys stand in place staring at us. We dance to one song; once it's over I decide to walk through the crowd back to where we left the two guys standing with Alicia, Leelee, and Connie in tow.

Sensing my discomfort, Alicia yells over the music. "Dee, this is Joseph. He is friends with Bryant."

I extend my hand to him. As we lock eyes I try to read him. *Does he want to acknowledge our past? And what about his brother? I should just say something.*

Joseph gently and ever so delicately shakes my hand. "How are you, Dee?"

Stiffening up, I grab his firmly. "It's actually Desiré. Only my friends call me Dee." *That was so bitchy.*

His face registers confusion. I don't think he could tell if I was joking or not. He looks first at Alicia and then back at me. "Oh I'm sorry I didn't mean to offend you."

"Oh, it's no problem." I finally tell him. *This is way simpler than I'm making me. I should just say something.*

When he releases my hand from his grip, he steps aside. "This is my younger brother Marcus."

This is when I hesitate. I can't bring myself to shake his hand so I wave at him quickly instead.

"You look really hot." Marcus says leaning into me. "You know if Alicia didn't tell me, I'd never know you weren't a real girl."

"Thanks." I say. *Welp at least you are still an asshole. Good thing I wasn't nice to you.*

Alicia looks at Connie and Leelee in horror. Alicia turns to me. "Hey Dee, want a drink? My treat." She says trying to change the subject.

I look away into the crowd of people dancing and shake my head no. "Milkshake" by Kelis starts blaring on the dance floor. I begin rocking back and forth to the music.

I finally blurt out "I think I'm gonna go dance."

Before anyone can respond, I sashay through the crowd again to the dance floor alone. I begin dancing to the music. Lost in the music, I don't notice a guy on the dance floor who begins suggestively dancing behind me. He grabs my hand and pulls me through the crowd then up on stage; we grind to another song playing. At the end of the song and the beginning of next, I lean into him.

"Thanks for the dance." I shout over the speakers.

I turn on her heels to leave; he tries locking his hands around my wrist, but I manage to stop him from doing so. I step down off the stage into the crowd.

When he sees me approaching, Joseph stops watching me and turns around. "I think she's pissed you told us."

Marcus chimes in, "Probably embarrassed we know. But hey, I would rather know beforehand than fuck her and find out like we're on *Jerry Springer.*" That shit is scary."

"That's exactly why I told you, Joseph." Alicia chooses not to respond to Marcus, but acknowledges his last statement. "She is a great girl really. You can't judge her for what she is, but rather who she is"

"Technically, she's not a girl," Marcus interjects. "She does drag."

"Dude, don't act like an ass," Joseph scowls.

"Hey what the fuck ever? She is acting like she is God's gift here. My bro Joseph here is open-minded enough to be set up with a transvestite."

"She is not a transvestite," Alicia corrects him. "They are people who dress like the opposite sex. She is a Post-Operative Transwoman, moron. She has had full Male-to-Female Hormone Therapy and all the necessary gender reassignment operations."

"Transvestite. Transsexual. Transcontinental; what the fuck ever." Cockiness exuded from Marcus' words. "Point is she is acting like she is doing him a favor by meeting him. She's all stuck up, nose in the goddamn air." He points to Joseph. "If you were trying to set me up with her, I'd say <u>HELL NO</u>. I could never be with someone who used to shave her face and pee standing up. That shit is nasty." And with that Marcus leaves.

Joseph laughs. "Sorry about my brother. He's ridiculous."

Alicia waves him off. They finally notice me standing behind Joseph; Alicia and Joseph stop laughing and stare at me.

Even to those close to me I'm a fucking joke. A punchline for some funny anecdote. I could feel the tears start to well up under my eyes. "I never felt like a freak, until now." Those were my parting words. I sprinted off through the crowd towards the front door.

I could hear Alicia's footfalls behind me, but I don't turn around. Joseph grabs Alicia by the arm

"Maybe I should go apologize for Marcus and all." He says.

I rush past the Bouncer in tears. He notices and puts up a hand to Joseph's chest as Joseph tries following me.

CHAPTER 10

As I run across the street not even looking both ways I see my car in the not so distant darkness. I instinctively fumble for my keys in my purse while walking with zombie-like formation towards my driver's side door. When I reach my car, I deactivate the alarm, and catch a glimpse of my tear stained face in the car window.

Fucking Marcus. I should go back in there and tell everyone how he hit me, how he big his dick really is, and most importantly how he likes his butt played with. I think to myself as I wipe my tears away. *And I should've acknowledged Joseph more. He was a big part of my college life.*

The sound of moaning behind me breaks my train of thought. I turn to look in the direction of the moaning, but see nothing in the darkness.

"Hello?" I call out.

I open the door and begin to climb inside, but hear the moaning again. With one foot inside, I sit in the driver's seat, throw my purse on the passenger's seat, and grab my flashlight from my center console.

Putting both legs back on the pavement I stand next to the open car door shining the flashlight in the direction of the moaning. Walking forward I find a toy on the ground that is making the moaning noise.

"What the fuck?" I say out loud before dropping the toy and sprinting back towards my car.

That's when I stop about three feet from the now closed car door. As I slowly walk to the car I hit the button to unlock the doors only they are already unlocked. I finally reach the door handle and suddenly a gloved hand covers my mouth from behind.

Not again. My head tells the rest of my body.

I immediately bite on the hand, but the figure backhands. The sting knocks me on my back. The figure flips me over on my stomach. *NO!* I keep thinking as I squirm trying to get away, but he grabs both my wrists with one of his hands. His other hand creeps up my skirt and rips off my panties.

"NO NO NO NO" I scream still wriggling.

I can break free this time. *I cannot be raped a second time.* But ultimately it happens. The pain of his thrusting inside me feels all too familiar. It's in that moment I realize I've had more rape encounters than I've made love with someone.

If I bleed to death here on this parking lot ground I will never have had the big love story of my life. I reason with myself while still struggling to fend off my second attacker. *I will never have had the chance to get married, adopt kids, own a house, go on vacation with my family, honeymoon with my husband, see my kids grow up, grow old with my husband. No. I will have missed all of that if I die here on this ground. If I can't get him off me I can at least will myself to live till tomorrow.* I close my eyes through all of this. *Dear God, I know I never reach out to you. I know I don't go to church. But I believe you exist. I know it. If you could please grant me the strength to live, to be able to wake up to a sunrise, I promise I will do everything in my power to make my life better.*

I whimper with every thrust with my eyes still closed. The rawness of his body in me begins to burn my insides. *When is he going to stop?*

"Until now. I always got by on my own." The figure whispers in my ear. And just like that I'm a statistic.

"They" whomever they are say whenever you are a victim of rape you know your attacker, even the masked attackers. This voice, that line. Could only be one person: Sloane. My whole demeanor changes. I'm angry. Blood boiling over angry. Something comes over me and I suddenly open my rage filled eyes.

I throw my foot up to hit him in the crack of his butt and he releases one of my wrists. Then with all the power I can muster I drive my elbow into his nose. Blood explodes all over my bare elbow and his face. He releases my other wrist and cups his nose with both hands. He falls back in screaming pain before bolting up to his feet and running away. I want to follow him and keep beating him up with my new found energy. But my body recalls that I was raped again…by Sloane.

With my body stuck to the ground I peel myself up and manage to get up to my knees. I use the car to balance while I stand on my feel. Wobbling to stand I open the car door wide. I slowly maneuver myself butt first into the driver's seat. Holding onto the door frame I try easing myself down knowing if I make a mistake I'd be in a lot of pain. When I finally sit down "a lot of pain" doesn't fully convey what I feel. I scream in agony with a sound out of me that I've never heard from myself. The pain is so excruciating I end up passing out with my legs dangling outside of the car as my body lies across the front seats. Even while passed out I can hear Joseph, Alicia, and the gang screaming and crying. Someone pulls me out of the car and cradles me. The sound of sirens tries pulling me out of my current state of sleep, but it's too late. I am in darkness.

My body feels light. I know I'm not dead, but I don't feel alive. Shocks pass in and out of my body; I think they are trying to revive me with a defibrillator, but I'm not sure. My eyes won't open to see. I can't get out of darkness. I decide to rest, just for a bit.

CHAPTER 11

T he beeping of my heart monitor wakes me up. I slowly force my eyelids open and realize by the TV mounted in the top right hand corner I'm in a hospital room. On the TV is the morning news; Matt Lauer greets Katie Couric. I look over to see Joseph asleep in a chair next to me.

I see a flash of a memory in front of me. I'm my boy self. Skinny, Black, and dressed awkwardly. As I walk on the campus of Western New England University for the first day of classes I try carrying my books in my hand. The banner on the St. Germain Building reads "Welcome the incoming Class of 1998." Joseph is off to the side of the banner joking around with his soccer buddies as I gawk at the big buildings. Between Joseph and his hackeysack and me not watching where I'm going he accidentally bumps me.

One of Joseph's friends shoves into me spilling my books on the ground. "Watch where you're going, Black faggot." He snarls at me.

Joseph pushes his friend. "Hey! Back off, racist homophobe. What are you in high school? Besides it was my fault" Joseph helps me collect my books. "You okay?" He stares through me like no one has before. For that split second it's just he and I standing on that stoop in front of the building.

Joseph suddenly wakes up in the chair next to me. He pulls off the white blanket covering his arms and stares at me.

"Wait, I know you." I finally say. "We met in college. I was…different then."

Still half-awake, he forces a smile. "Yeah, we met and had a few classes together through the years."

"Joseph Pagano." I pretend like it's difficult for me to remember. "Oh my god. I'm sorry I didn't recognize you before."

Stretching his back he settles back into the chair and smiles at me, "Yeah. You have changed a little, but those eyes haven't."

A silence befalls both of us. We both have so much to say but not enough words. The moment is broken by the presence of a tall-ish wiry guy with dark brown hair and a white coat. His name tag reads Dr. Van Tassel.

He asks me questions like do I know where I am, do I know what year it is, do I know what happened to me, and about the details of processing my rape kit. Dr. Van Tassel must've saw me roll my eyes.

"Ms. Andersen, everything okay?" He genuinely asks.

I chuckle. "I've been through this before okay? Process my kit. Do what you need to. But nothing will come of it."

Dr. Van Tassel sits on the bed near my feet. "Ok, Ms. Andersen, so you were raped previously?" He puts on his plastic gloves and begins moving my legs up pulling me from a sitting up position back to a lying down position.

"Yes. They said they didn't have enough evidence or some shit." I lean my head back on the pillow and open my legs. I grab Joseph's hand remembering how I hate this part. Joseph grabs my hand with both of his.

"You okay?" Joseph soothingly asks.

I begin to sob uncontrollably from pain of the examination from hopes this will be enough to convict Sloane from my whole world being uprooted once again. Joseph gets up, leans forward, and rubs the length of my arm. A Hispanic female Detective with her hair pulled back in a long ponytail comes in after Dr. Van Tassel is finished. She stands by the door with a stern face. She introduces herself as Detective Christine Cruz as I continue weeping residual tears. Joseph climbs in bed with me. I put my head on his chest.

CHAPTER 12

On the TV screen in front of my bed Neil Winters and Dr. Olivia Winters chat in her office on "*The Young & The Restless.*"

"Have you heard from Nate Jr.?" Neil asks Olivia.

"No. My son is incommunicado. Last I heard his stepfather Malcolm told me he's with Doctors without Borders in South Africa." She gets up and puts a file in a cabinet.

"Malcolm. How is my lil brother?" Neil inquires.

"Good. We've stayed on friendly terms since the divorce. And he's been amazing with Nate Jr."

Joseph walks into the hospital room holding two coffees. He passes the generic 2005 calendar on the wall by the door.

I put my head back on my pillow and think to myself. *What I wouldn't give to be on a soap opera.* I immediately think of Taylor. I turn my head the opposite direction of Joseph because I can feel the tears starting to well up out of the corner of my eyes.

"Detective Dones said you should contact her two days from now." Joseph says as he sits next to me putting both coffees on the end table by the bed. "Thankfully you get discharged today. I can't wait till you're out of here."

Having successfully stopped myself from crying I turn to him, "You and me both." I turn my head, reach over, and grab a coffee. He drinks the other.

Later that day we are seated at Ritchard and Kimberly's dining room table. Joseph sits next to me on one side with Ritchard & Kimberly sitting on the other.

"Why did I never sign up for drama classes in school?" I ask them while sipping the hot chocolate in front of me.

"Is that something you want to do?" Ritchard asks. The look on his face tells me what will come next.

"Because you know most of those actors struggle. And I love you so I'm going to be honest being a transwoman sorry a Black transwoman you think Hollywood is just going to create roles for you? Sweetheart, I'm not trying to crush your dreams but you have to be realistic."

"You two told me growing up I can be anything I wanted." I respond with a slightly crushed tone.

"You can, honey." Kimberly says leaning over and putting a reassuring hand on my hands. "But what your fath-Ritchard is trying to say is pave your way up. You want to be Meryl Streep...well sweetie, let me rephrase that cuz ain't nobody going to be Meryl Streep."

I laugh. "I will settle for being Hilary Swank."

"A two-time Oscar winner? Okay well see there you go." Ritchard looks at Kimberly. "Dream as big as you can dream, lil girl. Because you know what, you shoot for the moon, and you'll always win because you will end up amongst the stars. Just please take your time. Too many times these stars fade so quickly."

"I promise." I state crossing my heart.

In the hallway Monica and Rachel listen before running upstairs. In their shared bedroom Monica closes the door behind her. Rachel runs over to the desktop in the corner and logs onto YouTube.

"We doing this?" Rachel asks with her mouse cursor hovering over the "Upload" button.

Monica looking at the monitor answers, "Do it."

Rachel clicks upload, and there on the worldwide web for the world to see is me dressed in a gold lame gown (portraying Reva Shayne) yelling at Bryant in a wheelchair (portraying Josh Lewis) reenacting the classic fountain scene from the CBS soap *"Guiding Light"* in the Andersen backyard from three days ago.

Rachel and Monica found my high school monologue of this very scene (of course I was less Reva more Josh back then...at least physically) on VHS which sparked some sort of interest to film me years later. Oddly enough I went along with it, not knowing they wanted videos for their YouTube channel.

At their computer monitor in their bedroom, Rachel and Monica stare intently at the views.

"Come on." Rachel says trying to will the number up.

"Did you put in enough tags?" Monica asks reaching over the keyboard.

Rachel slaps her hand away. "Yes. Move. Wait wait look."

During the sixty-five minutes Joseph and I are downstairs talking to Ritchard and Kimberly (Alicia is in her trailer with her husband Damian; and Bryant is at soccer practice), the video of Bryant and I labeled "GL's Fountain Scene" gets five-hundred and eight thousand views. They scream and hug each other.

Downstairs we all look up at the ceiling. Ritchard shakes his head; Kimberly rolls her eyes.

I sigh. "To be a teenage girl."

CHAPTER 13

Over the next few weeks the strangest things begin happening.
First I keep getting these strange emails from SoapCasting.com about
wanting to talk to me about working in the soap industry and a phone
number. *Bunch of junk,* I think so of course I delete the email remembering that time
I went with Alicia and the kids to a modeling expo and they wanted us to pay for
our comp cards. But then four

more show up during the week in its place. *Man, spammers are aggressive these
days.* I keep pressing delete on the forthcoming emails.

Next up Lynette wants to promote me to Keyholder at Express. I can't believe
I'm still here. Working at the same job and my only prospect is full-time Customer
Service Rep. The alternative is quit this job and good luck to me finding another
job. When I came out they didn't fire me. They changed my name tag in fact, held
a meeting telling our store staff about my transition. Lynette (so I'm told) verbally
threatened anyone who had a problem with me and stated they would be fired on
the spot, but the thing is if I become a Keyholder aka full-time Customer Service
Rep I can stop paying out of pocket for my insurance. No more paying two hundred
dollar bills every six months for my follow-ups. Something to think about I suppose.

Third I haven't seen my black family now in over a year. I'm not sad at all. Maybe
it's because I have my white family, or maybe I'm just sick of the stress. Although I
don't see Alicia as much anymore since she's been married to Damian. I don't have
one hundred percent proof but I think he's beating her. I can't get the family riled
up without proof.

Speaking of relationships, the final and most odd thing that's occurred is Joseph
and I hanging out more and more. Whether we're enjoying a meal at Teapot in
Northampton by the Hibachi Grill, sitting under a tree on a full-size AIDS quilt
in Boston Common reading <u>Twilight</u> together, whale watching on a Hyannisport
Ferry Boat, lying on a towel on Hampton Beach under an umbrella, joining me at
the soccer game as Monica and Rachel cheer on the squad and clapping for Bryant's
goal, or walking hand-in-hand at the Holyoke Mall at Ingleside I find myself longing
for his presence on a daily basis. There was one time in my life I was like this…a
very long time ago.

Today at the mall he finds a bench in the women's section and sits down while I
go into the fitting room carrying clothes on hangers. I end up buying (with my secret
credit card Ritchard doesn't know about) a red Valentino butterfly-back silk gown

with red Naughty Monkey Candyland pumps, the white Diane von Furstenberg Pansy Ponte di Roma jersey dress I saw in the window, and a pair of Colin Stuart python print peep-toe pumps.

Later that night I walk into my living room, sits down on my couch, and cozy up next to him. It was in that very moment on my couch after all these months I realized out loud.

"I haven't met your folks."

He turns his head towards me. "What?"

"You know damn well you heard me." I say sitting up. "I haven't met your folks. We've been consumed with my family and my life. Not once have I met your family."

He begins to stumble.

"Are you ashamed of me?" I ask.

"No no baby it's not that." He says taking my hand with his free hand as he moves the hand that was holding my shoulders to rub my arm. "I'm proud to be your…boyfriend? I'm your boyfriend right? Cuz we never technically had that discussion."

"Yes you are. Don't try to change the subject." I brush his hand away from my arm and fold both my arms over my chest. "You know…" I want to tell him about Marcus and my past with him. But how do I do that? It's been months. The words don't leave my mouth. *Maybe I should leave well enough alone.* I lower my head and he runs his hands on the side of my face. He pulls me into a warm, apologetic kiss. It ends up being more than just a kiss.

I fix my hair in the bathroom mirror before adjusting my boobs in the Victoria's Secret black lace teddy I bought secretly while he was in Radio Shack. I flick the light switch off and see Joseph asleep in my bed. I giggle thinking about how this is like that scene in "Pretty Woman." I walk over to him and sit on the edge of the bed.

"He sleeps." I say with a smile before kissing him on the lips. Unlike the movie Joseph stays asleep, I turn off the lamp on his side of the bed, and walk around to climb into the other side.

When he senses me in bed, he rolls over, putting his arm over my stomach. He kisses my temple before we both enter sleepland.

Sitting at a wedding reception at the Delaney House in Holyoke, I tug up my tangerine strapless sheath dress. Then I notice a piece of lettuce on Joseph's lapel. I pick it off and smooth a hand down his grey pinstriped suit. Without stopping to eat his Waldorf salad he nods a thank you. Two female guests gush over my shoes, but I'm completely oblivious. The new Lynette Coleman dressed in her wedding gown comes over to hug me. Lynette shoos the shoe gawkers away. Her new husband Montgomery "Monty" shakes Joseph's hand.

The window fan blows in the morning air while Joseph lies shirtless and awake on his back in my queen sized bed. I'm next to him snuggled into that body nook with his arm around me. He smiles while watching me still asleep.

As I awaken, I look up at his face and am startled. "What are you doing?"

"Just watching you sleep." He whispers kissing my forehead. "Hey we should get to work soon. I am gonna go fix us breakfast."

"You don't know my kitchen." I challenge him.

He kisses my forehead again. "I will find my way." I lift up enough to let his arm free; he jumps out of bed and rushes to the kitchen.

I reach over to my night stand and grab my cell phone. I take the charging cable out and start dialing.

Alicia picks up on the other end. "What's up, Dee?" On the other end of the line she walks around her store.

"How'd you know it was me?" I ask.

"All cell phones have caller ID." She holds the phone away and shakes her head before bringing it back to her ear. "I'm the natural blond remember? So what happened?"

I begin to whisper before getting up to close my bedroom door a crack. "Joseph is making breakfast for us."

"Did you two-" Alicia starts.

"No. I don't think we are ready for that." I say as I climb back in bed.

"So what happened?" Alicia probes. "Did you two fool around?"

"Actually we haven't. He either falls asleep or I'm just not in the mood. Maybe I bore him."

"That is so cute." Alicia says as she rings a customer up balancing the cordless on her shoulder. "Well I don't wanna play the devil's advocate, but I do think it's sweet that you two are together and all. I had no idea you two met in college, and now this. You couldn't write that stuff."

"I know, but it's moving too fast." Desiré says. "I feel the same way as you do about the whole situation, but at the same time I want things to go slow. Leesh, he knows me. What and who I am, and he accepts me for that. He makes me feel so good about myself, and well that scares the shit outta me. And don't say I can't live in the past. I know I am still not fully over the rape, my bio family, and all the other shit that went on in my life even before all this. I just want a second to be alone and sit in my problems ya know?"

Joseph comes down the hall balancing a tray of breakfast food, but stops when he hears me talking on the phone.

Alicia continues, "I think he is a nice guy, but I don't know. My only thing, Dee, is knowing he's Marcus' brother after what Marcus did. I won't say anything to him; that's just weird. I wonder if Marcus said anything to him. " A brief silence gives Alicia time to do what she's good at: making a tense situation funny. "I know he's white and all but what if he's got a lead pipe in his pants."

"Jesus don't say that. Hey what if he is hung like a Tic-Tac?"

"Nah I heard he's big actually. He may rip you a new one."

The silence is deafening. Alicia tries to recover, "Oh my god, I didn't mean that."

"It's okay." I assure her. "I mean funny thing is I realize I was raped, but I don't feel like I was anymore. I don't feel that monster inside my body anymore; at this point I'm just dealing with the emotions of it. Ten points for the pun though."

"That was good huh?" Alicia chuckles to herself, but then stops herself. "Totally unpc but good."

"You don't have a politically correct bone in your body." I say. "Meanwhile I'd settle for any bone at this point." Then I hear the floor creak. "Joseph is coming back I should go. Talk to you later."

"Bye honey. I love you." Alicia says.

"Love you too."

As we hang up, I turn to see Joseph coming in the bedroom with a tray of food: sizzling bacon, four French toast triangles, six perfectly flat pancakes, two glasses of Orange Juice, a plate full of scrambled eggs, and a bowl of homefries.

"Thank you, babe." I say as I lean over the tray to kiss him.

He puts the tray on the bed in front of me, climbs in bed next to me, and begins eating the food with me. He turns on my VCR remote as we watch 'It Happened One Night.'

CHAPTER 14

oseph holds open the entrance door to the Enfield Mall as I rush in past him. We barrel past the four elderly people dressed in identical light blue sweat suits whom are speed walking. A young mother rocks a baby carriage back and forth as she stares into the front of the J.Crew window while drinking a coffee in a Starbucks plastic cup. Two older Asian men with "Maintenance" name tags assist each other changing the garbage bags of a trash can. I maneuver past Charlton, the overweight Middle Eastern Mall Security Cop, on his Segway with Joseph behind me. Just in front of Structure, Joseph pulls me back by the arm.

"Dee, I am gonna go to work; I will see you in a bit, ok?" He lightly kisses me. "Listen, take it easy. You're just a few minutes late, okay?" He holds me till I calm down.

I take a deep breath, plaster a smile across my face, peck kiss him back, and sneak past the customers into the back room.

Joseph walks briskly in the opposite direction of me adjusting his "Pagano's" apron. He scurries behind the counter into the kitchen. As he rushes past, an older version of himself closes the kitchen doors behind him. His father pushes Joseph back into the wall. Joseph glares at him with all the rage in his body. Suddenly Joseph charges at him clamping his hands around his father's neck. His father's head knocks down all the pots and pans hanging from the ceiling. Outside the kitchen patrons perk up at the sound of the brawl destroying the kitchen. Marcus claps his hands to the two Waitresses and a Cook whom stand paralyzed staring at the closed kitchen door. Mrs. Pagano moves to the kitchen door, but Marcus stands in front of her.

"They need to do this." He says as he walks Mrs. Pagano back to the front of the pizza shop.

They decide in silence to ignore the commotion and carry on business as usual.

In the Structure back room, Krissy dressed in denim cut offs with a plaid purple short-sleeved button down walks in. She pulls her bone straight jet black hair in a low ponytail while she walks to the office I'm in. The sound of her Chuck Taylor Converse sneakers scuffing the floor alerts me of her presence.

"Hey Dee." Krissy chirps.

I look up at her from the mountain of paperwork. I am about to say hi back, but despite her chipper greeting I notice a worried look on her face. "What is it, Krissy?"

Walking as fast as my legs can carry me without running, I finally make it to the front of Pagano's. Just as I am about to walk in, Marcus moves in front of me and ushers me to the side.

"Listen, now is not a good time." He whispers still holding onto my arm.

My eyes focus on his hand but slowly and eventually stare him back in the eyes. I can't read them like before. He must have noticed he was still gripping my arm because he let go.

"Oh, I'm sure you're just concerned for your brother." I finally muster.

Joseph's battered presence behind Marcus shifts my eyes away. Marcus follows my eyes, turns around, and sees Joseph. Without a word, Marcus leaves.

I move towards Joseph and gingerly touch his bruised eye. His head recoils in pain as he also takes a step back.

A step I immediately notice. "Oh, I see," I flatly stated.

"I'm so sorry…" He starts but the tears choke the rest of his words preventing him from finishing any explanation.

Standing in front of Joseph, I suddenly turn and walk away leaving him alone and bruised. As I slowly carry myself on my legs down the hall back to Structure I see a couple. The tall blond Caucasian boyfriend stands next to his short blond Caucasian girlfriend with his hand on her back as they look at sunglasses at a kiosk. *They look like what Ken and Barbie would look like if they were human.* The girlfriend tries on a crazy pair of sunglasses and turns to her boyfriend. They laugh as she checks herself in the mirror. I stop dead in my tracks for a moment to stand and watch them. *When do I get my love story? My happy ending? Why does everything have to be so fucking complicated? I deserve what those two have. Why is it so fucking hard?* I shove the rest of my thoughts down and meander towards Structure unaware the couple has walked ahead of me and is inside the store.

As I walk in my zombie state, I walk behind the cash wrap. Steven, dressed in a slate blue button down with rolled up sleeves and dark jeans, is ringing up the same couple I saw at the kiosk. At first I don't notice them as I'm busy going over hourly numbers, but then I get the feeling I'm being stared at; I look up from the binder. The couple stares at me. *How'd they get so far ahead of me that they selected and purchased something? How long was I standing there?*

Krissy comes up beside me and whispers, "You okay, sweetie?" Krissy takes the untagged items and heads back to the customer putting it in a shopping bag before smiling at them as they leave.

"Yeah." I response.

Steven hands the boyfriend his receipt; then he walks the couple to the front of the store. "And I'm Steven." Steven shakes both of their hands. "Thanks for stopping at Structure. Come back anytime."

As the couple walks past the Structure display window the boyfriend looks back at me. "Have a good one."

I instantly snap back into retail manager mode, "Thanks, sir, you too." I even add a wave.

Starting to walk out of my sight, I see the girlfriend nudge her boyfriend. At that moment something clicks, and I see the boyfriend's face as clear as day. It morphs from his smile at her now to his same smile as he danced with me at a club. *That's the guy from the club I danced with. He dragged me onstage and got pissed I left him.* I snap out of my trance and run from behind the counter to the front of the store. Standing in the middle of the mall with my hands on my head in both directions I no longer see the couple. *Could he have been the one that raped me? No it was Sloane. I know that.* I think to myself. Then I remember the reason I didn't want to finish dancing with him. In my head I hear the remix of "Alone" by Heart.

I walk back inside Structure defeated. I notice a tall blond slightly overweight man dressed in an EMT uniform sifting through the piles of jeans stacked along the wall near the dressing rooms. Using work as my distraction I approach him.

Like a robot I instruct him about proper size and fit. He's smiling, and then I realize he's blushing. After taking a few outfits to his dressing room, I walk to the cash wrap. He follows coming out of the dressing room with some jeans and t-shirts in hand. Reaching over the counter to take the items from him, I begin my Structure credit card sales pitch. He interrupts my usual spiel with his agreement to sign up.

I detach the bottom portion of the price tags on his purchase items, fold them into a neat pile on the counter behind the cash wrap, and move to the end register. "There are a couple questions I need to ask. First what is your name, sir?"

"Shayne Gomes." He says sliding down to the end register to her. "I know pale as a ghost. My dad's Brazilian; mom's Cuban." He rolls his eyes at himself. "What else you need?" He asks clearing his throat.

I punch keys on the cash register while looking at the monitor. "Last four of your social, please?"

"8267." He says quietly while leaning over the counter.

I punch more keys. "House or apartment number?"

"76." He says as he skims at the credit card brochure I put on the counter.

"Zip code?" I ask.

"01108." He is much more involved in the brochure now.

"And your phone number?" I ask as I finally look up.

"Is that for you or the computer?" He asks just as I see his skin go flush again.

I uncomfortably smile. "The computer." I look back down at the monitor.

"860-555-3344." He says while closing his eyes to remember.

"Ok." I finish and move from the register back to his purchases putting them in a shopping bag. "I am gonna start ringing you up while your credit check processes."

I scan the bottom portion of the price tags into the register one register down. The end register finally processes a receipt. I grab it, scan the barcode from the receipt to complete the transaction in the register. I hand Shayne the bag as the approval slip prints out. After he signs the receipt, I grab the pen along with a temporary credit card from the other register.

I write information on the temporary credit card pamphlet not looking up at him. "Ok, you were approved for a $1,500 limit. And like I mentioned, I took ten percent off this purchase today." I hand him the temporary credit card then take the signed approval slip from him.

"Cool. Thanks." Shayne places the pen on the counter. "Now I guess you will be seeing more of me." He again rolls his eyes at himself.

I smile as I place the approval slip in a drawer near the cash register. I notice the extra printout from the credit card approval at the end register, and hand it to him.

"Don't forget this. It has your phone number on it." I inform him.

"You keep it." He smiles at me before he leaves.

Yeah no. I wait till he leaves the store before throwing it in the waste basket under the register.

CHAPTER 15

K endall bounces up to the cash wrap in Structure to hug me. In heels we are the exact same height when we talk face-to-face. Kendall locks her purse in a cabinet behind the cash wrap; she then pushes her long auburn hair out of her way as if it's preventing her from fully talking with me.

"One day I am just gonna cut it all off." She says as we walk together out of Structure to the nearest Starbucks inside the mall.

Seated in front of me, Kendall beams and slides the Assistant Store Manager offer letter across the table in front of me. I take my time reading it like Ritchard has always suggested before smiling with excitement. As I smile I look up and clearly see the "Pagano's" sign. Kendall's chatter breaks my gaze. We walk back to the store separating when Kendall heads through the backroom door. I walk past the cash wrap, give Steven and Krissy a thumbs up who high-five each other, before putting the now signed letter in the cabinet near my purse. Kendall comes out minutes later, unlocks another cabinet behind the cash wrap, grabs her purse, and walks again to the front of the store with me as we talk.

While standing in front of the store talking to Kendall, I catch a glimpse of a bald very fit man slowly cruising by. *IT'S SLOANE! IT'S HIM! Why isn't he in jail for something? Anything? I will take anything at this point!* I think to myself while trying to concentrate on what Kendall is saying. As we continue chatting a bubbly blond girl runs up to Sloane, grabs his hand, and leads him away. I watch them leave and notice Joseph staring at us from the counter of Pagano's. Kendall tells me about her long ride back to Columbus so we say our goodbyes before I go back into the store.

Of two things I become sure of as I walk back with Kendall. One that I have to do whatever it takes to get Sloane in jail. And two that I truly am in love with Joseph, but my pride prevents me from fighting for him. I'd rather love him from afar than fight to keep him close. The Andersens have been my only constant; no one else has stuck around permanently including my black family. I'm too chicken shit to let Joseph stay.

After Kendall leaves I sit at the oak desk in the back office of Structure. I stare at the blank computer monitor before pushing in the keyboard drawer. Sitting back in the black leather rolling chair I look up at the two shelves above the desk. The first shelf houses three white binders leaning against each other next to the silver framed photo. Inside the photo is last Christmas' Andersen family portrait including me. On the next shelf up sit stacks of printer paper. I close the open metal file cabinet drawer next to the desk. I spin around in my chair and push back the black Queen Anne style chair set up against the wall. The chair somehow morphs into Joseph's face. Joseph's face then morphs into Marcus'. Marcus' face morphs into the boyfriend from the kiosk which morphs into Sloane's.

I shake the images out of my head and pull my chair closer into the desk. I open the binder on the desk marked "Policies and Procedures." The four men's faces cycle back and forth through my head now obstructing my vision. I can't think or see so I run out of the office into the nearby bathroom.

Staring at myself in the mirror, tears begin forming in my eyes. The mirror suddenly begins to splinter in front of me. The next images that pop in my line of sight are a box cutter, two bloodied wrists, and then blackness. *Ouch.* The pain in the back of my head gets stronger now that I'm lying on the bathroom floor. The images of the four guys are gone. I close my eyes and drift back into familiar darkness again.

The sound of banging on the door jolts my body on the Structure bathroom. The bright fluorescent overhead lights pierce my vision. I struggle to open my heavy eyes. *Where am I?* I hear the sound of my own name being shouted. Even though it's distorted I know the voice is a man. I roll over to my side on the bathroom floor, and things go dark again.

The sound of his voice again opens my eyes, but this time the harsh interior lights in the back of the ambulance stare back at me. I search around quickly and fixate on the EMT holding my hand. *Get that thing away from me.* I resist the oxygen mask with my free hand, but his one hand is too strong. Once the mask is finally on, the oxygen relaxes me. I smile at him through the mask; he smiles back and squeezes my hand. His lips move, but I can't hear what he's saying. I tilt my head to the left and look out the ambulance window. *Look at the streetlights move. They are getting blurry. Am I in a spaceship?* I close my eyes.

Still unconscious I can hear the man reciting into a walkie talkie. "June sixth. Patient suffering two self-inflected wounds to the wrists. Patient seems to be waking up. Will administer oxygen as levels are still low."

I decide maybe it's time to take another little nap. And just like that the darkness washes over me again.

CHAPTER 16

The TV is on in the background when the nurse comes into my hospital room. I stare at the "Macy's 2005 Christmas in July" TV advertisement while the nurse does her routine vitals check. The nurse ends her check-up by helping me take some pills with water. As the nurse opens the door to leave, Ritchard and Kimberly enter. Alicia, Bryant, Monica, Rachel, Kenneth, Deborah, Hayley, and Olivia are seated in the Waiting Area. Kimberly rushes over and hugs me while Ritchard cries behind her, hand over his mouth. I reach out to Ritchard who walks over with tears in his eyes to greet my hand with his. Outside in the hallway Joseph walks up still bruised holding a dozen carnations.

"YOU!" Bryant charges at Joseph.

The carnation bouquet falls to the floor as their fight knocks over a few nurses. The fight moves to the Waiting Area; within seconds Joseph's body splinters the coffee table. Security breaks up the fight dragging them to separate hospital rooms. Meanwhile Ritchard and Kimberly visit me in comfort oblivious to the commotion in the Waiting Area.

Dr. Barbour examines my wrists. He touches my knee, and I sit up.

When Dr. Barbour walks out, he motions for Ritchard and Kimberly to leave with him. They stand right outside my door down the hall from the melee.

"Desiré is going to be fine. They'll be minimal scarring, but no serious nerve damage was done; she basically nicked a small artery which we were able to repair." Dr. Barbour explains, "She is out of the woods, but I strongly suggest she begin seeing her Psychotherapist again. She is in the room resting comfortably after our exam, but for her own safety I did have to give her something." He pauses. "She flashed back to the attacks for a second she said and there was a recent breakup. I don't really know how to help as I'm not specialized in Psychotherapy. Might want to have her start there. She'll be groggy for a few hours, but you can take her home once the medication wears off in an hour or so. Okay?" Ritchard shakes Dr. Barbour's hand before Dr. Barbour leaves. Ritchard walks over to the EMT at the Nurse's Station.

Ritchard hugs him then pulls back. "The nurse tells us you saved her. Thank you."

"It's my job, sir." The EMT says with a smile. "She okay?"

"The doctor just said she was going to be fine." Ritchard shakes his hand "What's your name, son?"

"Shayne Gomes."

"You're SHAYNE?!" Alicia exclaims who has appeared along with Bryant,

Rachel, and Monica. The others are still down the hall catching their collective breaths.

Clearly taken aback Shayne replies, "Have we met?"

"Well no but Desiré talked about you." Alicia reveals.

Ritchard brightens up. "Why don't you go in and say hi, son? I am sure she would like to see you."

Shayne thinks for a second. "No I just wanted to make sure she was okay. Tell her I said hi though." He smiles before leaving.

CHAPTER 17

In my living room, Monica and Rachel share a seat while at my computer desk; they are looking through my emails on the desktop computer. Kimberly dusts the coffee table with a paper towel as she lifts up my laptop. Bryant channel surfs on the couch. Ritchard opens the door allowing Alicia and I to walk in before him.

I look around the living room. "Make yourselves at home." I laugh while walking over and sitting next to Bryant on the couch.

Kimberly walks over to the dining table with glass cleaner. "It's either that or you are coming home with us." She begins wiping a wet towel over the surface of the glass top.

"No. I am staying here, and you all are going home." I remind them as I make my way to a seat on the couch next to Bryant.

Bryant pushes a button on the remote turning the TV off; he faces me. "Were we not there for you enough?"

Silence befalls all for a second. I think long and hard before I break it. "What, Bry? Don't be silly."

Monica leaves Rachel at the computer and crouches down at my feet. "We are your family." She says to me. "We have been there for you through everything, and we will continue to be. Isn't that enough? Isn't that worth living for?"

"Yes of course. I love you guys so much." I say while hugging Monica by the shoulders.

"Then why the fuck did you do this?" Bryant spits. "What the fuck were you thinking? Did you give a shit how it'd affect us?

I turn to Bryant. "I was thinking about how to make the pain in my heart stop. I wanted to not feel anymore. It hurt so bad; I needed for it to stop. That was what I was thinking; I fucked up. I'm sorry; you're absolutely right this was a selfish act. I didn't think about how it'd affect all of you at the time. I truly am sorry."

The silence speaks volumes. No one says a word except the Gecko in the Geico commercial on the desktop computer behind Rachel. Kimberly finally stops cleaning; she walks over to me, whispers "I love you" before she kisses me on the top of my head. Kimberly then walks into the kitchen, puts the cleaner away, and grabs her purse before heading out the front door in tears.

"So um Rachel and I uploaded your video with Bryant on YouTube." Monica finally confesses. "We've gotten over a million views, and people from some soap opera casting company keeps contacting us to meet you."

"What? I thought that was fake." My face goes flush. "I thought that was spam."

"Oh no." Rachel says turning in my chair. "That's how a few soap stars got discovered. In fact there's this soap called "*The Pretty & The Powerful*" that shoots in Boston."

The shock of realization slaps me in the face. "Are you kidding me? I've been getting these emails from soapcasting.com and deleting them."

Rachel looks on the computer. "It says on '*The Pretty & The Powerful*' website that they cast through them." She slowly turns around. "Sorry we didn't tell you earlier. I guess we thought now…" She stops.

I nod understanding what she means. "I haven't watched that show since college. How funny is that."

"And darling, I don't do entertainment law, but I can definitely get a referral for you from some associates." Ritchard helps.

I sit thinking of the wonderful things that are about to happen to me. Everyone must've sensed it because they all stood up. Monica and Rachel hug and kiss me, then Kimberly and Ritchard follow suit. Bryant stands by the door and hugs everyone as they leave. Still in my daze I don't notice the nod he gives Alicia. She stands up, hugs and kisses me, then does the same to Bryant before closing the door behind her. When the door shuts, I notice Bryant is still here. I look up at him, and he saunters into my fridge, grabs a Capri Sun, and plots down next to me. I stare at him.

"Hook me up with one of your hot co-workers." He says while grabbing the remote control from the coffee table and propping his feet up jolting me out of my daze.

I laugh realizing I can't get rid of him. "I'm bad at playin cupid. Don't worry you will find someone."

He takes one of my throw pillows from behind his back, lays it across his lap, and pats it. I rest my head on the pillow as he channel surfs.

"So you and Joseph are done?" He pries.

"I think so. I don't want it to be, but I think so." I say as I watch him channel surf. "Will you pick a station?"

"There's nothing on."

"I pay Comcast about two hundred dollars a month to have all the channels. There better be SOMETHING you can watch."

Bryant sighs. "Oh wait I think '*Family Feud*' is having a marathon."

"Since Richard Dawson died the show really tanked for me. Is there a '*Law & Order SVU*' marathon on?"

"No wait I got it." Bryant exclaims. He presses buttons until he gets to '*The Pretty & The Powerful*' OnDemand. "Let's watch the past five days of this."

"Why?"

"Because what if you end up on this show? Don't you want to know the history and background?"

I suddenly recall all the times I spent watching '*Guiding Light*' with Taylor as a kid. I turn to look up at Bryant tears now fully flowing from my eyes.

"She'd want me to do this with you." Bryant leans down and kisses my forehead. "Besides I'm your brother I have to protect you and bug you about things you don't want to do."

I turn my head, wipe my tears, and begin our five episode marathon.

CHAPTER 18

My leg keeps shaking as I sit cross legged in the sterile white office. Behind me are the glass doors I entered through which muffle the sound of the bank of elevators "dinging." I'm sitting on the black leather Barcelona sofa across a stainless steel nomad square coffee table which is in front of an identical black leather Barcelona sofa facing me. All of the furniture is under a white faux sheepskin area rug which rests over the white marble throughout the floor. The pictures on the white walls are black and white images of Boston from the Public Garden, Boston Common, and Bunker Hill to the Old State House, the statue of Paul Revere, and Trinity Church. The windows are accented by white linen curtains that puddle to the floor. I nod my head looking around and notice the Receptionist has looked up from her book and is staring at me. She rolls her eyes then continues to read.

For some reason it didn't hit me before but the stainless steel desk the Receptionist sits at is probably the most interesting thing over there. Standard black quilted leather, but the desk, the only way I can describe it is looking like taking old radiators, flattening them, and bending them in desk shape and putting a filing cabinet and two long drawers mounted under it. Oh and a glass top covering the surface. I smile to myself envisioning the radiators heating up like I'm 'FireStarter' and melting the plastic inside the Receptionist. She'd be hair and eyes in a sack of bones on the ground. This sick thought makes me chuckle.

I clear my throat then primp my hair, which is teased out a bit but falls just below my shoulders in waves. I tried to find the most "soapy" outfit I could, so a magenta deep v-neck peplum long sleeve with a black pencil skirt and gold belt and pumps would have to do. No one else is waiting in the Audition Room at Soap Casting because there is no part being shopped.

"Desiré Andersen." As the receptionist shouts from the desk next to me, I jump.

I stand up and give her an evil eye but her face is buried back in her Jackie Collins novel. Walking down the white hallway passing three shut doors on each side of me till I reach the double doors at the end of the hall I turn around and realize I have to pee, but the hallway directly in front of the Receptionist desk feels like miles away.

Cork it, girl. I turn around, tighten up my entire body, and walk through.

Inside the white room is a long conference table matching the Receptionist's desk with the same black quilted leather chairs around it. There are no windows, but this time one big case with awards on the wall directly opposite the double doors and magazine and billboard posts on the other three walls. My snooping around didn't even notice the three people sitting directly in front of me. They all stand up.

Wendell C. Pierce introduces himself as the Executive Producer of 'The Pretty & The Powerful.' I gasp shaking his hand realizing I must be auditioning for a part. There was an authentic kindness in his handshake if a handshake could portray that. His salt and pepper messy short hair was accented by his blue grey eyes and just slightly tan skin. He wasn't overweight, but definitely not built. He looked like a healthy man in his fifties. His iridescent green Armani suit told me although he was older he hadn't lost his style.

Next was Sharlene Stoley. Her firm handshake was something she knew she'd have to get use to as the old saying goes "It's a man's world." Sharlene had sandy brown hair which she pulled back into a perfect bun. Her features could have been softened by just a few clicks of the magic wrist with a lil Avon in her hand. Instead her face came off harsh and unimpressive. She actually cracks a smirk at me while introducing herself as the current Headwriter of 'The Pretty & The Powerful.' I don't know if it was genuine or if she had gas, but I reciprocate.

The last hand is Wendell A. Pierce, Wendell's father and older self. They look identical save for Wendell A being taller by an inch, wearing black square glasses, and in a light grey suit. He nods as he tells me he's Head of Daytime Programming for BET.

We all sit after the introductions, and I decide to break the ice.

"Thank you for seeing me. I'm truly honored." I say not even knowing whom they are.

"Well thank you for finally answering that email." Sharlene spits even though you can tell she means it as a joke. "You are a very unique person. And such natural talent."

"Well thank you." I smile and nod.

Wendell C. folds his hands on the table and leans forward. "The reason we are here today is to not audition you for a role, the role is yours. But ask you for the opportunity to play a part." He pauses noticing my smile. "If you do not know 'The Pretty & The Powerful' is a daytime soap opera on BET. Our ratings since our debut fifteen years ago have not been all that great, but the network loves the writing and multicultural cast. My father thinks that's the reason why this show's been honored by Daytime Emmys, Soap Opera Digest Awards, and People's Choice Awards as you can see." He flourishes his hand behind him. "Oh sorry so we're on the third floor which is the Executive Offices. Second floor houses the production offices and the Writers' Room. First floor as you walk in to the left is our soundstages, dressing room, and obviously the building's cafeteria, gym, etcetera."

"Another reason why we're so invested in 'The Pretty & The Powerful,'" Wendell

A. chimes in. "Is that BET owns the show wholly. We want the show to succeed because we have invested our money into the budget and advertising dollars are ours."

I simply nod feeling like I may have over gotten in over my head. Without any warning the double doors open and Ritchard walks in. My eyes almost pop out of my skull.

"Sorry I'm late." He leans over shaking hands with everyone. "I'm Ritchard Andersen. Desiré's adoptive father, but also her attorney on retainer. I'll be representing her during any contractual negotiations offered." He sits down and puts his briefcase on the table. I still stare at him in shock.

"Well it certainly is good to meet you, Mr. Andersen." Sharlene says fully smiling. "So I received your YouTube clip a few months back and have been fascinated by your acting prowess so to speak." She's fully smiling at me now too. "So tell us about you, Desiré. This is your adoptive father. How'd you meet? Who are you?" She immediately reads the confusion on my face. "Well you as a person has a lot to do with the character and the show. You are going to be a newcomer to daytime onscreen and off."

"What she's asking is what are your dramas?" Wendell C asks flatly. "Are you a drinker? Sex addicted?"

I gasp and turn my head at how upfront these people are.

"Hey enough enough enough." Wendell A waves him back in his seat. "Listen, Desiré, what neither one of them is mentioning is the show needs you. We've tried matching our primetime counterparts being the daytime version of '*Desperate Housewives*,' we had an '*American Idol*' storyline, '*NYPD Blue*,' and we even had a medical arc to make us compete with that new show coming up '*Grey's Anatomy*.' Nothing has worked. So Sharlene thought of a great way to revitalize the show."

"Well I actually was writing the show back in the mid-nineties, stayed for six years, and left the business to deal with some personal matters." Sharlene folds her hands in front of her on the table. "Wayne here asked me to come back." She puts her hand on Wendell A's shoulder. "And I gladly accepted. But the show I once wrote is damn near unrecognizable. SO I decided I would do a whole coma thing."

"A dream thing?" I finally am intrigued.

"Back in the eighties the show '*Dallas*'...you remember it? With JR. Ewing and Bobby?" She waits for my fierce head nod. "Well they did a whole thing where one season Bobby got killed, and the next season he was alive and it was a figment of his wife Pam's imagination." She sees my intrigue. "Before I left the show I wrote a huge storyline involving Jillian Collins' character 'Molly' being shot and slipping into a coma."

"So the show would pick up with her out of the coma and you could rewrite certain storylines how you wish."

"Exactly." Sharlene smiles knowing we connected. "Jillian was previously a stage and screen actress locally here in Boston before portraying 'Molly' on our debut episode March 27, 1990. At first she was just the vixen and was supposed to last only four weeks, but her role was expanded when the creator whom were my parents just loved her. Actually when I mentioned personal matters it was their dual deaths that I had to come to terms with. It hasn't been easy, but I'm managing." She answered as if I had asked if she was okay. "Anyways one storyline that was near and dear to my parents' hearts was when 'Molly' befriended runaway 'Anita.' 'Anita' was a single mom desperate to not become the stereotype all Black single moms fall into. She and 'Molly' stayed friends throughout the show until her portrayer, also a stage actress Giselle Haywood, died of a heart attack last year. I think Wendell C expressly stated he's not looking to recast that role." Wendell C. nodded.

"And let me guess. 'Anita' had a son?"

Sharlene brightens up even more. "Her son was named 'Alan,' and he went off to war. We want to have him come back as 'Nina.' Thoughts?" She pauses crossing one arm over her chest while it props her other arm under her chin.

"Considering the fact that transgender characters have not been represented fairly in the media, I love this idea." Then the realization that I have never professionally acted hit me. "Wait I've never professionally acted before. How is anyone going to take me seriously?"

"And that is where I come in." Wendell C. chimes in. "I don't think it would help anyone to introduce you or your character to be background. We want you written as if you were a um biological female."

"With a love interest and stuff? No shit." I sit back in my seat.

"Exactly. But to be honest I don't know whom to pair you with." Wendell C. interlocks his fingers like a triangle in front of him.

"I was thinking 'Milo.'" Sharlene turns to Wendell C.

"Oh my goodness yes." He turns to Sharlene. "Brilliant idea." He turns back to me. "So 'Milo' is the son of 'Molly's' husband 'Jacob' and her arch nemesis 'Celia' played by Soliris Ortiz. Shar, you're seriously awesome. That would drive 'Molly' bonkers. We could have 'Nina' move in with 'Molly' and 'Jacob,' meet 'Milo,' have this whole forbidden love, and wow I think I actually have an erection."

"Oh for Pete's sake, junior." Wendell A. rolls his eyes; while Sharlene cackles.

I finally turn to Ritchard whose face never falters throughout this entire conversation.

"Now, hon," Wendell A. continues. "I've seen a lot of people crash and burn coming into the business. We need to tell you a few things before you say yes which we hope you do. First off the pay for a newcomer to daytime is roughly $100,000 per year. You agree to work for the show we can sign you to a standard three year contract and you'd have three to five days of work guaranteed. Now I know $100,000 per year sounds like a lot of money, but don't go spending it crazy. After taxes and your attorney's fees you're looking at roughly $40,000."

"A year?" Reality hit. "So wait because he's my attorney I have to pay him what 20% commission?"

"Yes. An attorney or talent agent needs to represent you plus you need a manager who also gets 20% commission." Wendell A. recites. "Point being don't go buying that Ferrari and new condo in the high rise. Keep a level head."

I turn to Ritchard who's writing down notes from a pad in his briefcase. "So why would I need a manager? I'd be living off of $20,000 a year from $100,000. No I will stick with just my dad." I see Wendell C. do a fist jerk through the glass table. "And I guess I will just move to Boston instead of traveling back and forth from Western Mass. And Wendell A., my car runs just fine. I won't be getting rid of her." He smiles. "As far as a co-star."

Hunter Bentley opens one of the double doors. As he walks in shaking everyone's hand I notice how muscular he is without being a meathead. His perfectly whitened teeth sparkle under his full lips. When he turns to shake my hand I could feel my knees buckle staring into his piercing blue eyes. After shaking my hand he does the international guy signal that he's interested in me: he runs his fingers through his hair. I smile, close my eyes, and nod. As I open my eyes I run them from his feet to his eyes. This man is the living version of the sculpture David.

"So I'm Hunter." He says sitting down next to me. Ritchard leans over to hear him speak. "I've been with the show for about two years. I was modeling in..."

"The Karl Lagerfeld collection. That's where I know you from." I snap and point to him. "Oh my God this is cray." I cover my mouth. "We are going to be love interests?" I giggle.

"I guess so from what I'm hearing." He blushes. "I will say it will be my honor playing opposite you. And don't freak out when we kiss. I can't do a Hollywood kiss." He does the air quotes. "I'm all about French. Come in for the real thing with me. You know what I'm sayin?" He laughs which makes me laugh.

"I love the chemistry between you two." Sharlene says leaning in. "This is going to be a joy to write for."

"Hunter, why don't you take Desiré on a tour? Show her the ropes while we talk shop with her attorney, Wendell A suggests.

"It would be my pleasure." Hunter says darting up and holding out his arm for me.

I stand up, grab my gold clutch, and interlock my arm in his. He holds open the door for me but still interlocks our arms.

CHAPTER 19

"**S**ome of the shit they won't tell you," Hunter begins, "is that no matter how successful you become in the soap world we're out on our own." He continues. "The rest of SAG, that's the Screen Actors' Guild that helps manage our working conditions think of it as OSHA but unionized, anyways if the rest of SAG goes on strike, namely Primetime and Cinematic Actors, we have to. Which is a great show of solidarity, but they treat us like garbage." A new side of Hunter emerges. "We learn 75 pages of dialogue in one day. We have what - a couple hours of blocking. We put up with fans attacking us personally more than other celebrities yet we don't get a category at the SAG awards, Golden Globe awards, and we barely make it at People's Choice awards. People keep trying to blame O.J. Simpson on the destruction of daytime. Fine he helped, but when the daytime community faltered and no one stepped up to acknowledge we were dying that's what put the nail in our coffin." He pauses to look at me. He cracks a smile realizing how intense he's coming off. "Sorry I know you're new to the business, but I'm not some dumb model. I know what's up. I've done my research, and any of the real actors that sell out movies and win Primetime Emmys are either theater trained or from soaps. So don't go paying for an acting coach; you wanna learn Acting 101, study the other actors in their scenes particularly Jillian Collins. That woman is a living legend. She's been dubbed the Meryl Streep of Daytime because she's literally that good. She's actually excited to meet you too."

We walk into Soundstage 3, and everyone yells "Welcome" with a banner "Welcome, Desiré" hanging across the Director's booth. I'm completely taken aback and cover my mouth in shock. Jillian is the first to walk up and hug me.

"Hi dear, I'm Jillian Collins." She puts her hand on my back and guides me away from Hunter. "This is Soliris Ortiz. Our costume designer Sheleen White, Blaine Benton who plays 'Zane,' and I think you know Jenica Hughes." Jillian says Jenica's name with the biggest grin.

I hadn't fully registered what she said all I saw was her face. My shock went to tears as I burst with excitement, ran to meet Jenica, and hugged my childhood friend in the middle of Soundstage 3.

After hugging for what felt like forty years she pulled me away to look at me. "Look at you. Little Elijah Davis, all grown up." I still can't speak. "I rendered you speechless. Oh man you shoulda seen her when we were growing up. Motor mouth.

She got kicked out of class once for talking too much." Jenica hugs my shoulders. "So good to see you, my friend."

"What the fuck?" Is all I could muster.

Everyone laughs.

"There you are." Jenica laughs. "You haven't changed. And by the way you owe me big time, sister." She continues without waiting for my "What the hell for?" "Because who do you think showed your video to Sharlene? I had heard you transitioned of course from my mom who still lives in Pheasant Hill Village. I guess they somehow got to talking to Rachel, who sent them your video, who sent it to me, and boom. Mic drop." She pretends to drop a mic.

I stare intently at my old friend. She's still blond hair and blue eyed, but she doesn't look like a normal actress. As we talk she tells me after she and Landon (she married another Pheasant Hill kid) had their twins she couldn't lose the weight. The soap wrote her pregnancy and battle with weight in. She decided after getting letters from every fan imaginable to simply be her and not lose the weight to fit Hollywood standards.

"I'm just not into that shit. And don't you get sucked it. Girl, I'd kick your ass if you did." Jenica texts on her cell. "Landon is demanding dinner today after work. The three of us."

"Done." I say.

"Wait, you have a place in Boston yet? If not you're staying with us. We have a guest bedroom."

I perk up even more. Then Hunter sits down at the 'Molly' & 'Jacob's' dining room table with us.

"I have a good feeling about you, Dee." Hunter says.

"Thanks, Hunt." I reply. He smiles before leaving. "What's his deal?"

"I've been here ten years and I still haven't figured him out." Jenica continues texting. "Seems like a good guy. Isn't into partying or skirt chasing. Very serious about his craft. Always prepared. We call him One-Take-Hunt. He nails every line in one take."

"Well I'm not looking to start drama. He'll be my work crush and that's it."

"Good idea. OH MY GAWD Wendy just told me we're sharing a dressing room."

"Who's Wendy?"

"Wendell C. Pierce. We call him that cuz his dad named him Wendell fucking C. Not Wendell A. junior.

Fucking Wendell C. So annoying. Wendy actually likes his nickname. He's as awesome and odd as how you met him upstairs by the way." Jenica hops up. "Come on let's move you in."

Jenica shows me first our dressing rooms. It's basically two small bedrooms with a Jack-n-Jill bathroom. Then she takes me to the cafeteria to meet the kitchen staff whom everyone knows by name. We see the gym, indoor pool, library, and we pop into some other soundstages. I accidentally almost spill Leonardo DiCaprio's coffee on him. He apologizes for some odd reason.

Sitting at the vanity with my back to the mirror I look around the pretty plain room. There's a quilted yellow fabric sofa resting over a yellow/grey/white/black Chevron patterned area rug, a high end cherry oak coffee table with magazines on it and a remote control, a plasma TV on the wall next to me, after that a door with a hook (my name on the other side. And along the wall of the bathroom door is a closet with sliding mirrored doors.

"I want to paint that one wall grey and leave the rest white." I speak out loud thinking I said it to myself in my head. Feeling comfortable enough when Jenica smiles I continue. "And I think I should find that poster from when we were kids and met at that rubber band fight. I'm pretty sure someone's parents took a picture of us fools." Jenica starts laughing. "And my picture with the Andersens will go here." I get up and plot my wall displays.

"How's your mom and brother?" Jenica asks with a chuckle.

I am sure she was just remembering the good times growing up together with that gang of kids we had. I turn to show her my disapproving face at her mentioning them. Her face drops immediately. "No it's okay. How could you have known? I haven't spoken to my black family in a year. I've been only in contact with the Andersens."

"Oh my goodness Alicia. Her and her family are such good people. I'm so glad you had them this whole time." She stretches out her hands to me. I lock mine in hers as she pulls me to the couch to sit next to her. "I am so sorry."

"No it's okay. Really. I am better off."

"And how's everything else? Are you dating anyone?" Jenica asks with a look of guarded concern. I think she doesn't want to say the wrong thing again. I simply smile.

My cell phone lights up with "Mom."

CHAPTER 20

Ritchard and I drive in silence on our way back to Springfield. The three-year $100k a year contract was signed with '*The Pretty & The Powerful.*' I will begin work in two weeks and gonna crash with Landon & Jenica till I find my own place. I just got off the phone with Structure, and they understand. They aren't happy, but at least they get it. This could be my chance. Steven was promoted in my place instead. Ritchard said he'd pay the rent and electricity on my place till I find a place and am able to move my stuff. He said it's cheaper than renting movers twice and putting it in a storage unit. I want to be excited about everything that's happening, but all I can think about is Kimberly's call.

The twenty foot Christmas tree twinkles with multicolored lights dead center in the lobby at Baystate Medical Center. In front of the tree is "Santa's Workshop." One male elf ushers a little boy up to Santa's lap; while one female elf manages the line. A father with his wife and two toddler sons walk into a toy store. I hold open the front door for an elderly couple pushing a stroller.

Ritchard and I speed walk to the all too familiar bank of elevators and take it to the third floor.

Getting off the elevators I walk up to the Nurses' Station with a visibly shaken Ritchard behind me. "What room is Alicia Wilson in?"

The group of nurses stop talking, one approaches me, and tells me with a sympathetic voice "Room 313."

I turn around and for the first time in my life see Ritchard about to fall apart. I instinctively grab his arm and walk us both to Room 313.

I open the door with one hand and prop Ritchard up as we walk with the other. Alicia breathes on a ventilator. Bryant paces at her feet. Kimberly holds her hand in the seat in front of us, but hearing our footsteps turns her around. I can see she's aged in the last hours of this.

She gets up and hugs and kisses me and hugs Ritchard pushing him back and crying out. I walk forward, and Bryant falls apart in my arms. I walk him to the seat on the other side of Alicia then lean over to her.

Kimberly unburies her face from Ritchard and walks over to her original place next to Alicia. She grabs her hand and talks in a louder than normal tone. "Alicia, honey. Desiré is here. Honey, your sister is here."

Alicia tries opening her one good eye. I reach down and slowly touch her hand; she squeezes it.

Bryant shakes his head. "He broke two ribs, fractured her eye socket, broke her left arm in two places, and shattered her clavicle." Tears fall from his face as he looks out the window.

Ritchard walks behind Kimberly and puts his hands on her shoulders. "And where is he?"

"Prison. The DA says he won't make it out of prison." Kimberly manages to admit through tears.

"I wish he'd just do us all a favor and kill himself." I say out loud walking over to grab the tissues. I come back to Alicia and blot under her good eye.

Monica and Rachel enter behind Ritchard with food from the café. They smile at me and hug Ritchard.

Out on the sales floor Shayne walks into Structure, up to the cash wrap, and sets bagels down on the counter. Finished with his customer, Steven scurries to the cash wrap up to Shayne. Krissy, who is standing nearby, walks over and opens the bag; Steven goes to the back room door.

"Dee, you got a visitor." He yells.

I give Lynnette a hug, pack up my box of personal things from the office, and walk to the front. That's when I see him. "Hey." I say.

"Hey how is it going?" Shayne says to me.

I set my box down on the counter and notice the food he brought. "You didn't have to do that. Thanks though."

"No problem." Shayne says. "So I hear this rumor this is your last day. Figured I'd get a last day 'hey I saved your life' dinner."

"You?" I realize. *It was him? Wait did he see my medical records? Does he know?* "Why are you so set on going on a date with me?" I ask. Steven and Krissy are within earshot but so focused on eating they ignore us. Still I move to the side of the cash wrap away from them.

He moves closer to me. "Have you ever met someone who just fit everything you were looking for?"

"No." I continue. "I don't think I'm in a position to meet that person or be that person for someone else."

"Well I think I have, and I want to take her out on a date to see if this is real or not." Shayne says smiling. "And before you say anything Boston is an hour and half away. It's not California."

I stare at him trying to figure out what to do. Push him away by telling him the truth. Be horribly mean so he hates me. Tell him I'm just not ready to date because I'm not over Joseph. Give him a chance cuz maybe he's not like the rest. "I have a lot of baggage right now. It's just not the right time."

"Well we can always discuss that over dinner." He persists.

Tell him at dinner. I look away from him unsure of how to proceed. I finally look back at him. "Fine. Meet me at Ruby Tuesday's at nine tonight."

"It's a date." He says with a huge smile before leaving.

I wait till he's fully gone before gathering my box and trying not to cry as the crew walks me out of the store for the final time. Lynnette hugs me and tells me to keep in touch. Steven hugs me and tells me he loves me. And Krissy holds my bag of items she, Lynnette, and Steven bought me. She says she wants to walk me out to my car to help me, but I know it's really to flirt with Bryant. She saw a picture of him on my phone and has been obsessed with me introducing them ever since. We walk to his car in the parking lot and sure enough they hit it off.

Later that evening, Shayne walks up to the Hostess Station at Ruby Tuesdays. She escorts him down the aisle past the Garden Bar to the table I'm patiently seated at. I stand up, hug him, and sit back down in my seat. Shayne almost hits his head on the Tiffany lamp hanging off center above our booth before sitting down across from me. He stretches out his legs under the table and takes his cell phone out of his front pocket to set it on the table. The hostess hands him a menu. As I take my menu from the hostess I glance down at myself and realize I'm wearing the purple Structure wrap dress. That outfit I wore to see Sloane at Mazda of Agawam. I can hear the muffled tone of a voice and look up to see the hostess is talking to us.

"Your waitress Isabel will be right with you." The hostess leaves.

"Wow I can't believe you showed up." Shayne says through a grin.

I respond, "Hey I told you it's my favorite restaurant."

Isabel approaches the table in the standard uniform of Black long sleeve button down, pants, and shoes. She takes the pen out of her dark brown bun as Shayne and I look up from our menus. Without a stitch of makeup but with a warm smile I swear this waitress could be a Victoria's Secret model.

"My name is Isabel." She says in a not perky but not hating her job tone. "I will be your waitress tonight. Our specials tonight include Shrimp Scampi on Fettuccini with a light yogurt cream sauce, a Fresh Lobster Roll, and Seafood Caesar Salad. If you have any food allergies let me know. But what appetizer would you like to start off your entrees with?"

I go back to the menu. Shayne looks up at Isabel. "Cream of Broccoli and Cheese soup and Salad Bar with a Corona with a lime please."

"Sure." Isabel writes this down then turns to me. "And for you?"

"I will have the salad bar too plus a Strawberry Lemonade with a lemon please." I close the menu.

"Absolutely." Isabel smiles while taking both menus from us. "You can go up to the bar at any time. I will have your drinks for you right away."

As Isabel leaves, I lean over the table looking into Shayne's eyes. "So I need to tell you something. I don't wanna scare you off."

"You won't; don't worry." Shayne grabs her hand with both of his.

I hesitate "Shayne, I am a transwoman."

Shayne pulls out a gun and shoots me dead. I snap out of my gaze at the table. He stares at me. "Okay I don't think daydreaming is good on a first date."

I apologize. "Oh my goodness I am so sorry."

"It's ok. I bored you. It's my fault." Shayne jokingly retorts. "How about we just go up and get food?" He smiles.

I grab my purse as he grabs his phone, and we head to the salad bar. With our plates full, we get back to our table where our drinks are waiting. We talk while we eat.

After we are done eating Shayne pays for the meal waving me away as I go into my purse.

Outside in the mall parking lot Shayne walks me to my car.

I notice him hovering. *Is he moving in for a kiss?* "You know I actually had a better time than I thought. That's not a slight to you, but like I said I've had a lot going on lately. I just wanted to thank you for making this a great night, but I think this is all just too soon."

Shayne grabs my hands. "Desiré, if you should learn anything from all of this it's that life is too short to be resting on your laurels. You gotta grab it by the cajones."

"I got mine removed I thought I told you." She says hoping he'd pick up on the reference.

"You're too much." Shayne laughs "Well how about I come visit you in Boston? I don't wanna push, but selfishly I don't want you to get away."

"Okay." I finally realize it's time. "So I do have something to tell you." I release my hands, and his face drops. "Do you know what a transwoman is?" He shakes his head no. "Ever since I can remember I've wanted nothing more than my inside self to reflect my outside self. Growing up as a little boy I-" I notice he takes a step back, but I continue. "Didn't feel gay, but I didn't feel straight. It was this weird middle. Growing up into a teen I realized I liked guys but not gay guys, and then it occurred to me I was born in the wrong body. I have had the gender reassignment surgery and so now I am a transwoman. I'm not trying to lie or mislead you. But that was part of the reason why I have been kind of standoffish with you."

Shayne's face is cold. "Well I'm not gay."

That was the moment I realized guys like Shayne will always exist. They hear me say transwoman and no matter what my explanation is they are immediately turned off. Part of me is sad realizing I will have to go through this over and over. Part of me is angry he got my hopes up he'd be different. And part of me is relieved to be rid of the hopes of me and him. "I see." I respond equally as cold. "Well thanks for dinner. Good luck in the future." I don't even shake his hand before getting in my car and driving off. I realize I buckled my seat belt with my purse on so I pull over to the side of the road, turn off my car, unbuckle my seat belt, take my purse off, and bawl for ten minutes. I compose myself, rebuckle myself in, turn my ignition, signal that I'm turning left into the lane, and drive into traffic.

I walk through the front door into the Andersen living room and see Ritchard in his lounge chair reading the local paper. Kimberly washes pots and pans with Rachel in the kitchen. Monica does her homework at the dining room booth table.

Bryant comes downstairs. "Hey sis." He walks over and kisses her on the cheek.

"Hey lil bro." I respond by hugging him before he goes into the kitchen to make himself a bowl of cereal. I stand looking at this family of mine and smile. "So I think we need to officially be a family." I say which turns everyone's head towards me. I move to the booth in front of Monica with all eyes on me. "I met with my Financial Advisor today to set up my life insurance, 401k, and devise a tax plan with my new income. And when I got to the beneficiaries part I realized legally Dorothea and Dorian would have medical clearance or be my next of kin. I can't have that. You all have been there. You all are my family. Hell, look at the family portraits, I'm in those." Everyone turns towards the row of pictures starting from the top of the hallway down. The first eight or nine don't have me in, but after the tenth I am there even up to the one we took last year.

"You're right." Ritchard says with a sigh putting his paper down. "If Kimberly and I legally adopt you as an adult, you do realize you will need to have your mother give up parental rights. I know it sounds odd, but it's the legal process."

"And you need to meet with her." Kimberly adds walking over drying her hands. "This is not something anyone should have to do over the phone or what not. You do this in person and be one hundred percent sure."

Bryant exclaims, "Holy shit-"

Ritchard walks over and smacks Bryant in the back of the head. "Language. Kimberly is right. If you truly want to do this I will draw up the papers and go with you"

"If I do this. I have to do it alone." I tell them. "You raised me to be a strong person. I can do this. How soon can you draw them up? I have two weeks to get myself situated in Boston."

"I can have the papers drawn up tomorrow." Ritchard states.

Bryant comes over to hug me. "This has been a long time coming huh?"

"It has." I kiss him on the cheek and hug him back. "And I wanna take Alicia with me."

Monica and Rachel smile. Bryant kisses the top of my head. Ritchard and Kimberly side hug each other.

CHAPTER 21

As I close my compact at the country kitchen dining set I look around at the apartment I left what feels like decades ago. Same butcher's rack with the microwave in it sitting on the wall next to me near the wall phone. Same country kitchen china cabinet that matches the table. And same checkered area rug underneath me. In terms of section 8 housing Pheasant Hill Village wasn't a bad place to grow up, and the residents had a flair for decorating. I chuckle at how dumb I sound in my head.

Dorothea walks in with a box and puts it on the square table. "Don't open this till you leave okay?" She half commands me like she's still my mother.

I roll my eyes. "Mmhmm. Anyways here are the papers." I push them across the table towards her.

She sits down and puts on her glasses hanging from around her neck. "I know I haven't been the best moth-"

I put up my hand in annoyance. "Stop right there. This isn't about you and your shortcomings as a mother. This isn't about Kimberly and her overcompensation as my mother. This is about what I want and need at this point in my life. I need you to sign those papers so I don't have to return here for any fucking reason whatsoever. I don't want you or him or anyone from this fucked up twisted family in my life. I want to be legally, physically, and mentally done with you all. I don't care if it hurts your feelings or pride. I don't give a flying fuck if you feel disrespected. None of you have been where I need you which is right at my side. So fuck you. Fuck him, and fucking sign the documents so I can get the fuck out of here. NOW!"

The tears burst from her eyes like a dam breaking. They drip into her glasses while signs the papers. I grab the signed papers, put them on top of the box, and march towards the back door a few feet away. She opens it for me. She is about to talk, but I cut her off.

"You've got nothing I want to hear." I continue walking to my car.

Once inside I start the car and drive off. I ignore the chiming in my car, drive through the first stop sign, and turn left onto the main entrance road. I park the car opposite the Pheasant Hill Village sign. I am about to put on my seatbelt to end the chiming when I decide to stare at the box. I move the papers next to the box in the seat, and open the box. Inside are my old journals, her old journals, letters, and pictures. I shake my head before replacing the top on the box, putting on my seatbelt, and driving off with Pheasant Hill Village in my rearview mirror.

I sit inside my car in the Andersen driveway with the engine running. I look over at the box. "We Belong Together" by Mariah Carey plays from my speakers as I reflect on my life in Springfield.

Being raped twice, working at Structure, meeting both Joseph and Shayne, old memories of my first love Jaxson, my life with my white family, my life with my black family, meeting Hunter and being at '*The Pretty & The Powerful*' set. My entire life floats in front of me like clouds in the sky. I'm trying to grasp everything. A knock on my passenger side window dissipates all the clouds. I look to see Kimberly who lets herself in. She picks up the box and rests it in her lap as she sits down next to me with the door ajar.

"Whatcha doing in here, hon?" She asks like a mom should.

"Just thinking about things." I respond looking out my window.

"I know a lot has been thrown at you recently, but you are such a strong person you will get through it all. And if you need help ask from us. We're your family."

With her last sentence I reach down on the floor below her to get the papers she knocked down when she sat down. "She signed them." I hold the papers in my hand and look at Kimberly.

Her reaction is a mixture of relief and sadness. I think relief that now I'm officially an Andersen, but sadness knowing it means I was unwanted by my blood relatives. I smile at her to assure her I'm happy, but a tear still manages to sneak out from the corner of my eye and she knows. She stands up, sets the box back down, closes the door behind her, and rushes over to my side. I turn the car off, take the key out of the ignition, step out, and fall apart in her arms with my door open.

CHAPTER 22

I put the car in park and turn to my right. Alicia is in the car with me as she turns to the right as well. We stare without words at what will be our new place together. 49 Woodbine Street, Apartment 3. A honk behind us breaks our concentration.

Getting out of my car we walk over to the U-Haul behind us. Landon & Jenica climb out. Landon smiles at me as the four of us move to the back. Just then two more cars pull up behind us. Ritchard, Kimberly, Monica, and Rachel emerge from one; while Bryant and Krissy emerge from the other.

"We didn't need a gang to help. It's a two bedroom apartment with literally 1 all purpose room and a bathroom." I say climbing into the back of the U-Haul.

"We just want to help." Kimberly says while climbing in herself and handing Monica and Rachel items.

Over the next three hours we unload the stuffed U-Haul and my car into the two bedrooms, bathroom, and multi-purpose common area. The common area is a kitchen, dining area, and living room about the size of a bedroom. We can fit our flat 45" wall mounted TV, cherry oak entertainment stand, three matching cherry oak bookcases filled with DVDs on one of the three white walls and just next to it a small square cherry oak table with four matching bar stools. Kimberly sewed bar stool cushions by hand in the same fabric as our crimson red quilted sofa bed. Opposite that wall is said sofa bed, cherry oak coffee table, red white and blue diamond patterned area rug, and one blue quilted accent chair with matching ottoman which is under the double window. Across from this area is a small walkway then our one-sided galley kitchen with 3 sets of wall cherry oak cabinets, our stainless steel microwave mounted under the stainless steel four burner gas stove, our stainless steel double sink with white subway tile backsplash, and our stainless steel side-by-side fridge with icemaker and water dispenser. As I stare in marvel at our efficient use of space Alicia throws a six foot long red white and blue striped runner down the walkway between the kitchen and living room/dining area in front of me. I turn to her, and she smiles.

"Feels like home already." She says. I walk into her bedroom to the right on the same wall as the sofa. Ritchard and Bryant put her bed together. Kimberly hangs up her clothes. Monica and Rachel move a bureau in place across from her bed. Landon sets the makeup table down behind Kimberly with the chair. Alicia grabs me by the waist and hugs me; I hug her back. Jenica squeezes past us and puts a box near Alicia's makeup table set up on the far wall near the closet.

"Behind you.' She alerts Kimberly. Landon grabs the box from Jenica.

Thirty minutes later after setting up my bedroom we all walk as a group down the streets of Quincy to The Great Chow. As we enter the Chinese restaurant we're warmly greeted and seated at a makeshift large table. We spend the next hour and a half laughing about old Pheasant Hill Village memories, discussing Alicia's new job as a Billing Rep at Columbia Gas of Massachusetts as well as her pending divorce and restraining order, and my new gig at *The Pretty & The Powerful.*

"You know." Jenica covers her mouth while she talks so food doesn't fly out. "Acting on a soap is a test in patience. What you told me Hunter said to you is all right. You really do need to have a thick skin and just deal with people. Fans especially. They get so enraged by a story it can bum you out like when my character was pregnant by a man she met at a bar. The story was the man and she were going to bond over the baby and eventually marry. The fans went so crazy writing letters to Soap Opera Digest and Soap Opera Weekly the network fired the man, my character lost her baby and ended up reuniting with her boring ex." She continues eating.

"The fans shouldn't dictate a show. That's awful." I say.

"It also has to do with the writers." Landon adds. "That old regime was so scared to go against the grain. I don't think Sharlene will put up with that crap. She seems very headstrong."

"I was talking to Wayne and her about Dee's story, and they are both fully committed and onboard." Ritchard says before shoving a fork full of shrimp lo mein in his mouth.

"If you are nominated for any award, Mon and I are your dates." Rachel states. She high fives Monica with her free hand as one hand helps her devour a crab Rangoon.

"I think I'd take Bryant or Alicia." I correct her. When I see her face drop I change my answer. "Okay maybe for like the Soap Opera Digest awards I'll take you two clowns."

Everyone laughs.

"So wait." Landon clearly is thinking out loud. "Ritchard is your attorney and represents you legally, but do you have a manager?"

"No I don't have enough money for that."

He turns to look at Jenica and nods. "Well I mean I'm Jen's manager I don't mind being yours."

"Oh thanks but I couldn't afford you. Seriously I cannot live off of $20,000 a year in 2005."

"Girl, I will manage you pro bono." Landon eats, looks up at me, and waits for my reaction.

"Pro bono? You'd manage my career for free? No I couldn't."

Jenica sighs. "I told you she wouldn't."

"What about ten percent until she gets an increased salary, and we can renegotiate?" Ritchard reasons.

Everyone thinks for a second.

"I'm down for that." Landon agrees. I nod as well.

Living off of $30,000 a year in 2005 doesn't sound SO bad right?

"And trust me you won't be living off of $30,000 a year for long." Landon says as if he's reading my mind. "Jenica is very comfortable with being on the show, and taking care of our little one. She does appearances here and there. But you are single, fresh to the industry, and I can see it in your eyes you're hungry. Mark my words I am gonna make you the next it girl in Hollywood."

"Okay but one thing. I do not want to move out West. And I have to meet Joan Rivers before one of us dies." I demand.

"Let's have a meeting tomorrow and go over your career plan. We will map all this out before you even start next week."

I smile as I sip my Wonton soup.

CHAPTER 23

I stretch dressed in my workout clothes on the yoga mat at the gym with Alicia next to me. A well-built dark haired man trains an older slightly overweight Black woman. The music from the Zumba class is heard even with the door closed. Two blond housewives wearing pearl necklaces ride stationary bikes in their yoga outfits side-by-side while talking and watching "*Good Morning America.*"

After we're done working out and changed I hug Alicia before leaving the gym. I walk down the hall to my dressing room. As soon as I close the door behind me and set my gym bag down a knock is made at the bathroom door. Landon walks in immediately after.

"So you ready for our meeting." He asks me before closing the door behind him and sitting down next to me on my couch.

Landon tells me that I need to hire someone hungry to be in the business pro bono to be my Personal Assistant. We both think of Alicia as it will keep her mind off her troubles. I tell him I will call her after our meeting. He thinks I should get on MySpace and have a profile; MySpace is this new social media website. He feels my presence will show how relatable and accessible I can be. Of course I protest telling him I don't want to overshare too much.

"Think of this." He hypothesizes. "If you share a beach pic or date pic before the media they got nothing. Think about it. The paparazzi can't hound you for pictures if you've already taken them. And we need to make them personal as all hell."

"I see your point. But back up." I remind him. "Date pic? Who am I dating?"

"No one right now. Okay listen what three things do you think will never happen in your lifetime?"

"A black President. A transwoman as a romantic leading actress. And Michael Jackson and Prince will both die before me."

"Interesting." Landon says sitting back on the couch. "So I think you're wrong on all three. But this is good. I am happy to prove you wrong on at least number two which I can control. So let me ask this question if you could date anyone in the world right now whom would it be?"

I don't even hesitate. "Matt Damon."

"I heard Jarnel Jeffries."

I look at him completely confused. "Jarnel Jeffries? The football player?"

"Exactly." Landon sits back up. "He plays for the New England Patriots. He's best friends with Tom Brady. They just won back-to-back Super Bowls last year and this year. He's single, black, and a Boston native. BAM" He laughs at my confused face and touches my chin. "So adorable. Listen no one expects a black transwoman to date a black straight guy especially an athlete that's why it's perfect. You don't know this but in Hollywood..." He opens his folder and shows her. "They have Confidentiality Agreements. Couples are always pairing up through their agents or managers. Some of Hollywood's biggest couples didn't meet on-set or at an awards show. No they were arranged through various paid associates then fabricated to make regular Americans want the life. The whole point of being a celebrity is to be adored and worshipped. You my friend, will be adored and worshipped. We will need you to have five things to become a major A-list celebrity: 1) Talent. 2) An enviable lifestyle. 3) High profile scandal 4) Love story. 5) Back story. These are the essentials to your rise to fame. If at any point you want to back out I promise you communicate that with me and we will."

"Okay but Lan, what about the haters?" I stand up and grab a water bottle from my mini fridge. He waves away my offer to get him one.

"Haters would exist whether you're a biological woman or a transwoman. Not going to lie yours will be more since we are going against the norm. But you know what, I guarantee you in ten years from now things will be vastly different. People are scared of change, but the only constant in life is change."

"Okay Confucius, settle down." I say sitting back next to him. "So what if Jarnel doesn't want to date a transwoman?"

Landon laughs. "He was involved with a rape case last year. He was found innocent don't worry, but it's left a bad taste to some. Trust me he will go for this. I will call him after we're done. And honey, I love you, but as soon as possible we need to upgrade your living situation."

"Okay so how am I supposed to afford a brownstone on Newbury Street?" I annoyingly ask.

He thinks for a second. "Okay we keep you where you are for now. Your persona is down-to-earth, every day people. You aren't hiring a stylist, or a makeup artist, or buying a Mercedes. In fact I'm going to contact Toyota to see if I can get you a free Prius." He smiles. "They are these new hybrid safe for the environment vehicles. They debuted a couple years ago. Trust me, you being an eco-conscious celebrity will get you far. And you will be shopping at second hand stores and online. No designer labels. Alicia can help you with makeup. Maybe we can even get you a deal with Avon. See you go small to go big eventually."

I'm amazed. "Wow you're good."

"It Girl. That will be you." He taps his temple. "We need a tag for you. Madonna is the Material Girl. Princess Diana is the People's Princess. You are the It Girl."

I chuckle. "More like the Ice Princess. I feel so cold and emotionless inside lately."

"Shh don't you even think that. You are not an ice princess, and I will never ever refer to you as that." He grabs my hand. "Since we were kids I always knew something was different about you. I never judged you or made fun of you. I loved you as my friend regardless. You know that. What I was certain of is that you had the biggest heart of anyone I ever met. You were one of my best friends then and you still are. You are not an ice princess at all. You understand me." He hugs me and kisses my cheek. "No I'm gonna call Jarnel's people. You call Alicia." He walks away on his cell.

I really did luck out in the friend department. I think to myself as I call Alicia, whom I know will agree to be my unpaid Personal Assistant.

CHAPTER 24

Back Story.

I walk up to the podium at the gazebo in the Boston Commons. I turn to my left and see Jarnel smile at me and wink. I look out into the sea of paparazzi and press below.

I look down at the speech Landon and I slaved over the night before. "My story is common. In 2006 it is still legal and socially acceptable to fire, bully, and beat up a transwoman. In my case I was raped. Not once but twice by the same man. The-" I pause and turn to my right. Landon nods to me. I continue. "The Springfield Police Department know the man whom raped me not once but twice. They have his DNA, but yet the DA for that district refuses to prosecute him making it okay for men like Sloane Williams to become repeat offenders or rape and attacks not just of transwomen but women in general. I have no idea if I was his only victim, but I am his only one willing to stand up and say enough. This man-" my voice begins to crack. "Date raped me then stalked me a year later and raped me in the parking lot across the street from a night club. He punched me and put me in a coma. I went through two rape kits. And survived by the sheer love and support of my adoptive family. My boyfriend Jarnel has been an amazing support system as well. I am coming forward now not just to expose the corrupt workings of the Springfield Police Department and District Attorney's office, but to any survivors of rape you are not alone. You can survive anything. He may ravage your body, but do not let him ravage your spirit. Thank you."

I walk down into Jarnel's waiting arms. Landon brushes off the questions as I walk through the gazebo's back entrance into the waiting limo. We wait for Landon to climb in before we drive off.

Landon turns on the TV in the limo.

"Giuliana DePandi. I am standing here live in Boston where actress and trans activist Desiré Andersen just announced her attacker. I think people had been waiting for some background on her and boy did we get it. I am truly amazed by her strength of character and sheer will. Unfortunately she took no questions from the press, but her boyfriend football player Jarnel Jeffries whom was accused of rape two years ago was seen crying while she spoke." They flash a picture of Jarnel wiping tears away. I look over at him, and he grabs my hand and kisses it. "I'm truly amazed by her strength. And Desiré, if you're watching, call me. I would love to sit down with you. Back to the studio." Landon turns off the TV.

"We did it." Landon high fives me.

"Baby." Jarnel seductively says. "I gotta go to practice. Meet me later at my place okay?" He kisses me on the cheek before the limo stops. He gets out and paparazzi swarm him as he ascends the stairs of his Newbury Street brownstone. The limo weaves in and out of traffic, one way streets, and red lights till we get to Club Café a few streets away.

Owner Jim walks Landon and I towards the far left corner where Ritchard, Kimberly, Alicia, Bryant, Krissy, Steven, Monica, Crasso, Rachel, Grammy, Grampy, Kenneth, Deborah, Hayley, Olivia, Jenica, and baby Lana are seated. Hugs are made all the way round then something tells me to turn around. Standing in front of me are a teary eyed Jennifer and Jessica, Jenica's moms.

Jennifer is an older version of Jenica in the facial features, but thick bone straight blond hair and almost sky blue eyes. Jennifer's plain white button down and tan khakis with tan moccasins accentuate the amazing figure of a woman in her mid-forties. I push her away to see her pink scarf belt and she tosses her hair.

"I got to keep up with you hot young girls." She says with a laugh.

"Don't hog her, Jenny." Jessica chimes in as she hugs me tighter than any normal woman should be allowed. I look at Jessica whose curly copper red bob and emerald green eyes make me wonder if Jessica and Jennifer somehow scrambled their eggs together before Jennifer carried Jenica. It's totally uncanny how Jenica is half of each of them. Jessica's style is much more upscale than Jennifer's with her green lace slip dress falling just to her knees and green and gold scarf draped over her shoulders and modestly covering her chest. Jessica extends her arms and forces me to look down at her green strappy sandals. To look at them you'd never guess these women live in an immaculately maintained section 8 housing project. But the reality is their combined salaries of social worker and Spanish translator really didn't afford much more than slightly above the median poverty line. "I know I'm not Jennifer, but come on. This body." I throw my head back laughing.

The servers bring us Standing Pork Loin Roast, Gourmet Mashed Potatoes, Homemade Gravy, Stove Top Stuffing, White Cheddar Macaroni & Cheese, and an open bottle of 53 Margaux. We are all laughing, eating, and talking about all the same subjects we do when we get together. This time Jarnel and my rapes are additional topics. As we are winding down Ritchard begins lightly tapping his fork to his glass.

"Before we leave," he begins. "I just want to take this time to speak on a subject we haven't talked about tonight. I know we've talked about a lot, but as of noon today with the presiding Judge Arnold Phillips, Desiré Taylor Andersen is legally the daughter of Ritchard Thomas Andersen and Kimberly Evalina Andersen."

Everyone cheers, and Kimberly hugs me while she cries.

"Welcome to our crazy family kid; I love ya, darling." Dad blows me a kiss.

I stand up pretending to cry now. "I don't know what to say. I don't even have a speech prepared." Everyone laughs. "Seriously though this has been an amazing journey. We are going on almost twenty-one years of knowing each other. I can't believe this is happening. You told me as a kid I could be anything I wanted. I simply wanted to be your daughter. Now that I am your daughter I demand you guys update your wills cuz I want mom's porcelain doll collection." Everyone laughs again.

"Oh no way, sister. I've been eyeballing that collection since I was like three." Alicia interrupts. "I'm the oldest so those dolls are mine."

"Um well technically. I'm the oldest now." I corrected her. Bryant starts the "ooooooooooooh," and Alicia fake cries. I hug her and kiss the top of her head.

I use my credit card to pay the meal. Dad sees and gives me a look like "Don't you dare." I give him a "I already did" pout, and he blows me a kiss.

We gather in front of Club Café and all hug each other.

I wake up in my bed with Bryant and Krissy cuddling next to me. I tiptoe to the bathroom and walk a little further to peek into the living room where mom and dad are snoring in unison on the pulled out sofa. I tiptoe into Alicia's room where Steven and Monica are in sleeping bags on the floor near the closet, and Crasso and Rachel are sleeping next to Alicia in bed. Crasso stares at the ceiling awake with Rachel in his arms. He notices me peek in and slides out of position, grabs something from his carry bag, and tiptoes out of the bedroom to join me in the kitchen. He walks me into the bathroom with him with something behind his back.

"Listen" he whispers in his slight Lebanese accent. "I am so sorry what Sloane did. So after I heard what he did I may have taken this from the inside security video." He hands me a dvd from behind his back. "Sloane can defend himself from your words, but he cannot from his actions." I hug Crasso before he tiptoes back to bed. I quickly pee while staring at the DVD.

A few days later I am on set at 'The Pretty and The Powerful' dressed in a sequined one shoulder magenta Bob Mackie gown, my hair in a messy bun on top of my head, and dripping in diamonds. I'm holding a glass of champagne standing at the table full of my cast mates. I turn to my right towards Camera A and Jillian at the end of the table.

"I would like to make a toast. To Molly. My second mother. Thank you for inviting me into your home and your heart." I say before sipping from my glass.

'Milo' bursts in - everyone looks to my left and at Camera B. "And I would like to make a toast." He grabs 'Jacob's glass from the other end of the table. "To Nina, you are the love of my life." He sips the drink, throws the glass, walks over to me, and kisses me in front of everyone.

"And cut." The director yells.

I pull back from Hunter. "Oh the shit's about to hit the fan now." Everyone laughs including Hunter. I look up from laughing with everyone to see Wendell A. and Wendell C standing behind the director.

I am being mic'd up while sitting in a director's chair in front of a camera with the E! logo on it. Everyone is huddled around a TV set nearby.

"Giuliana here back with E! News. We are going live to Boston where Desiré Andersen is patiently waiting. Desiré, how are you sweetie."

"GIULIANA!" I exclaim. "I am so happy to talk to you."

"Yes. Me too. I wish it was under better circumstances." She keeps the conversation on topic. "How are you handling all of this with the video of Sloane and you coming out."

"I feel like finally justice will prevail. They can ignore DNA and my word, but they cannot ignore video. They tried to say it was consensual and maybe I regretted, but I always told them from day one it wasn't consensual. Now I feel vindicated in my story. And I feel a dark cloud has finally been lifted."

"As the story breaks I hear not only was he arrested for your assault, three more women including his cousin have filed charges against him."

I go deaf in that moment. I cannot believe what she just said. My shock turns to surprise. "This is so much bigger than me." I choke on my words. "I don't know how that video got released, but I sure am glad it did."

"Well after all this is over we must have a sit down." Giuliana states.

I wipe away tears. "Yes I will meet you at Spago's and we can have dinner before our interview."

"You're on. Thank you so much, Desiré, for your bravery and perseverance. You are truly an inspiration."

"Thank you, Giuliana." I wave.

"And we're out." The cameraman says.

I throw the mic down without thinking and burst into tears rushing towards my dressing room. Jenica and Hunter trail behind.

CHAPTER 25

Love Story.

A group of kids nearly knock Jarnel over running by us at the movie theater in Copley Square. He's about six three and his skin is the color of a cup of cappuccino. "Light skinned brother" is what he'd be called. He's built like a football player obviously with broad shoulders, a full back, and thick legs. Surprisingly his waist is slightly thinner than you'd expect on a man with a forty-two inch chest and hips. And he dresses like a thin man. Tight straight leg pink khakis, a white turtle neck hugging his ridiculously muscular chest, and a white cable knit cowl neck cardigan hanging just below his waist. As I look up from his tightly faded haircut, perfectly sculpted eyebrows, hazel brown eyes, and full lips down to his outfit I settle on his tan suede desert boots. I shake my head at how beautiful this man is. As I look back up to meet his eyes I notice even his ears are perfect.

"So you approve." He jokes before touching my waist.

"Yeah you look gorgeous." I say.

He smiles with the whitest teeth I've ever seen. I don't know whether this is part of our Confidentiality Agreement or if he truly likes me. Whatever the case I lean in and kiss him. He kisses me back.

A line snakes in front of the Box Office. Jarnel points towards the open box office booth, and we walk up. At first the teen doesn't recognize us until he does. I turn as he talks to the teen and watch a father yell at the running kids. A customer service manager talks to a ticket taker. I walk over to browse the movie posters on the wall: 'Harry Potter and the Goblet of Fire,' 'Star Wars Episode III: Revenge of the Sith,' 'The Chronicles of Narnia: The Lion, The Witch, and the Wardrobe,' and 'War of the Worlds.' Jarnel pays for the tickets, grabs the receipts and tickets that print out, and walks over to me. We walk up to the ticket taker, and Jarnel gives him the tickets.

The ticket taker rips off the theater portion of the ticket. "*The 40-Year-Old Virgin*. Funny movie. Theater 3 on the left. Enjoy the movie." He says as he hands Jarnel the remaining portion of the tickets.

We stand in line in front of the Concession Stand.

"No I don't want to choose seats that you hate. We do the snacks and seats together." I tell him. He kisses my temple.

We order a large popcorn no butter with two large drinks and Sour Patch Kids.

When I go to pay he puts his debit card up. I look at him, and he again kisses me pushing my hand away from my purse. He grabs the drinks and Sour Patch Kids; while I grab the popcorn and some napkins. He smiles at the bag of Sour Patch Kids.

On set at the gravesite I turn dressed in dark denim rolled cuff True Religion jeans and a white rainbow tee under a black fitted J.Crew blazer on my pink sling back Jimmy Choo heels to see "Molly" standing with "Jacob."

"I'm sorry who are you? And why are you putting flowers at my friend's grave." Molly asks me.

I stumble on my words. "Um I----"

Molly moves closer. "Alan? Is that you?"

I nervously try to look away but I can't. The camera zooms in on me. "My name is Nina now."

"And cut." Blaine yells. Everyone claps. Blaine walks over to congratulate me on a job well done. I tell him he's an excellent first time director. Jillian hugs me before she's pulled into a debate with Sheleen if she should or should not wear a turban in her next scene.

I wave bye to everyone and walk to my dressing room. On the way there I say hi to various crew and cast I see along the way. I walk inside and notice the bouquet of multicolored roses in a glass vase on my coffee table. I grab the card:

No reason, just wanted to say hi. Don't be late tonight.
Love,
Jar-Jar Jeffs

I smile getting his reference. Jenica busts through the bathroom door.

"Come quick you do not want to miss this." She grabs my wrists and drags me through our shared bathroom and into her dressing room where Landon is glued to the TV upset at what he's watching.

"I'm Giuliana DePandi, and welcome back to E! News. Take a look at this." Across the screen is a picture of Jarnel kissing me at the movie theater. "Unequivocal proof Super Bowl winning football player Jarnel Jeffries is dating soap star transsexual Desiré Andersen. Todd, what are your thoughts?"

Todd Newton is now onscreen. "I mean it is a nice departure from the normal big chested bimbos he dates. But a transsexual; it's transwoman, Giuliana. I don't know. Back in 1997 Eddie Murphy was caught with a transvestite prostitute, which is different from a transwoman. But there's been such a bad stigma to the transcommunity. They are always on 'Jerry Springer' and years ago 'The Ricki Lake Show' as the butt of a joke. From what I hear Desiré is an upcoming actress and pretty sweet lady. I dunno. I feel like we need to know more about her before we can categorize her."

"You're absolutely right. And my apologies I didn't mean to offend her or anyone else. Transwoman." Giuliana corrects herself. "It's still terminology for me at least that's new and I think a lot of people."

Jarnel's brand new Lexus pulls up on the dirt road. I look around at the scenery.

The sun reflects off Lake Squam in the distance making the water look as if it's shimmering. Trees abound only parting to show me houses, boat slips, and beach. Next to his parked car is a small brown two-story cabin with a matching brown shed. I didn't notice Jarnel has already gotten out and has opened my passenger side door. He extends a hand, which I take and climb out. He closes the door behind me, opens the back seat door as I marvel at my surroundings, and grabs our bags. We walk around from the side to the front of the house along the paver path to the screened in front porch.

"HEY HEY!" Comes from the man who's basically an older version of Jarnel. His father leaps from his seat, opens the porch door, and walks down to bear hug Jarnel.

"Hey pop." Jarnel struggles to say under the weight of his father's hug.

I look up to see various women and men sitting smiling at me...smiling VERY big.

"And this must be Desiré. I'm Darnell, Jarnel's father." His father releases Jarnel, comes to me, and clasps both my hand in his. His warm smile forces me to hug him.

On the porch I meet Jarnel's aunt Ophelia and uncle Kreston and their son Kennard, Jarnel's mother Jarrika, and his sister Darrika. His sister's boyfriend Vishon arrives later. All of them hug me deep and smile at me as if I have the Golden Ticket to Willy Wonka's Chocolate Factory.

The porch is decorated with two tan wicker couches, a matching loveseat, and recliner. Glass coffee and end tables with Tiffany mosaic lamps, a Lake Squam plaque, and two oars crossed together finish off the porch.

Finally at dinner I can't take it anymore and give a subtle jab. "You know growing up gay and then discovering my gender identity, it's just amazing Black folk talk to me...let alone have a cabin by the water."

Everyone laughs. "Well." Darnell begins. "The cabin was given to us two generations ago on my side. My great-great grandfather was the slave of a man who lived in the south. When he and his family died in a fire, it all became Great-Great Grandpa Tee-Bone's. Tee-Bone because he could cook a T-Bone steak like nobody's business." Everyone laughs again. "So Great-Great Grandaddy sold the plantation in Georgia, moved to New Hampshire on Lake Squam. He wanted to be as far from anyone else as he could. Built this cabin with his bare hands. Winterized it too so he could live here year round, I don't recall how he met Great-Great Grandmother Mabeline, but they found each other and here we are all these decades. The cabin stays in the family without question. It's so beautiful on a summer's day like today."

"And the family is definitely supportive of transgender people. Look how they treat me." Darrika smiles.

This is when I realize their smiles and complimentary attitudes weren't odd or weird, they were happy there was another transwoman in the family. Darrika grabs my wrist, takes me through the glass front door, and into the living room where a small fire burns in the brick fireplace.

The living room is just as cozy as the front porch. Wood everywhere. The ceiling is white with the beams their original wood color. One of those massive circular multicolored braided rugs lines the floor under the taupe sofa I'm sitting on across from the matching taupe loveseat. I run my hand over the wood coffee table with spindle legs and turn to see both the sofa and loveseat are both flanked by matching end tables and gold candlestick lamps. I then notice Darrika isn't sitting next to me, but Vishon comes in smiling at me and sits on the loveseat across from me.

"She'll be right back." He says. Just then she appears with photo albums in her arms.

Over the next half-hour I see pictures of their family when Darrika was Tevant. He was every bit the feminine skinny boy that I was; Tevant and Elijah woulda been best friends. I probably would've had to fight Jarnel though as Tevant and Jarnel were inseparable in every picture. The cute years being only two years apart in age, the awkward middle school years, and the high school morose phase. Best friends. Cabin pictures, home pictures, birthday parties, weddings, family reunions. She shows me pictures of T-Bone and Mabeline as well as various family members. She finally shows me the last photo album. Newer pictures of Darrika. A Certificate of Name Change. Copies of her Social Security card and Driver's license. And finally her wedding photo. It's in that moment I notice Darrika's ginormous engagement ring and sparkling wedding band.

"We haven't decided on kids yet, but who knows." Vishon confirms.

The rest of the family trickles in gathering around and even sitting on arm rests with Jarnel sitting next to me.

Jarnel puts his arm around me and leans back. "So how do you deal?"

For a second I think he's talking to me, but looking up from the photo album to see he's talking to Vishon.

"Deal with what, brah?" Vishon replies.

Jarnel looks at me quick then back at Vishon. "Being a straight man and dating a transwoman."

Everyone stops and looks at Vishon including me.

"Well excuse my French ma and dad, but I don't give a fuck." Vishon has prepared this speech I can tell. "I met Darrika at a club. We hit it off, brought her back to my place, and well you know." He looks at Darnell. "I'll spare you the details. But I found out she was trans. Man I freaked the f-heck out. Kicked her out and told her she was a freak."

"You didn't tell me this." Jarrika says to Darrika.

"Mama, shh. Let him finish." Darrika knowing the story wants to wait for the end.

"So anyways I was a bad dude back then. Partying, drugs, yo I was getting in it." Vishon continues as Darrika moves from the other side of me to sitting next to Vishon. He puts his arm around her waist when she sits. "Then one day I was pulled over in Wellesley, MA on my way to work. This cop was all up on my shit yo. Asks for my license and registration. I start freaking out thinking great I'm gonna be this statistic and die on the side of the road from police brutality. I was straight buggin. Five minutes later cop comes back asks if I knew my car insurance expired two days ago, he needed to impound my car. He asks me "Do you have anyone to call to come pick you up?" I was so embarrassed. I may have been a bad dude but always took care of my finances. The only number not my friend's in my phone was Darrika's. So I called her and explained the situation. Man I cried on the phone with her. Turns out coincidentally she was getting out of the movies at the theater not even two miles up the street. When she came to get me yo I cried like a bitch. The cop was telling her what I needed to do to get my car back, but I was all on her. Crying and stuff. Not cuz I was embarrassed anymore of that I am an emotional guy, but I realized that even though I treated her the way I did she was there. Nobody else was. I grew up in the system yo. Foster family after foster family. No one wanted me. And this girl right here." He grabs her hand and kisses it. "She answered my call and came for me. I'll never forget that day. Never. So to answer your question, Jay. I don't care what society or other people think. I found love and that kinda love you read about in romance novels and see in movies. I found the one person I know loves me at my worst and wants me to be my best. She's my everything. And when you find that it don't matter if she is transgender or not transgender. You feel me?"

Darnell clearly never hearing that story stands up in tears and hugs Vishon. Jarrika follows suit. Jarnel looks at me with loving eyes and leans over to kiss my cheek.

We eat lunch in the dining room, go on the boat with Vishon and Darrika while the rest of the family congregates on the porch drinking Moonshine and talking shit about other family members. The tour of Lake Squam from the boat is glorious as we even see the house where *On Golden Pond* was filmed. We meet some of Jarnel & Darrika's childhood friends…they call Lake friends. We attend an impromptu cookout, and some of their friends quiz me on *"The Pretty & The Powerful"* business. I always catch Jarnel just staring at me. When we are done visiting, we board the boat again, and head back to the cabin.

At night up in the loft we settle into bed. I'm wrapping my hair in the mirror and notice Jarnel has pushed the two twin beds together and hops in one. I smile as I put tie my silk scarf and climb into bed next to him.

"So." I state snuggling into that nook next to him under his arm. The smell of his naked skin is heaven.

"So." He responds kissing my forehead.

"I thought this was just going to be a contract relationship. You know to divert press from the rape things."

He pauses. "I thought so too. But I like you. Your personality is on point. I dunno. It's crazy right? I can honestly say we have SO MUCH fun. It's crazy."

"I love you too." I don't know why I said that but it came out.

He moves his head as I move mine up to look at him. "I love you. I really do."

There in the twin beds in the loft above the living room Jarnel and I make love for the first time. It's not the primal instinct attraction sex. It's the sex I've waited for my entire life. The kind of sex you want to be your first. The sex that erases every shred of the rapes from my body. The sex Vishon and Darrika probably have. I love Jarnel with every fiber of my being. And the three orgasms he gives me prove that. When we make love in the morning I tell him he doesn't have to use a condom.

After breakfast Jarnel and I hug everyone as we leave. Vishon and Darrika are leaving too; I exchange cell numbers with them and hug them one last time. We climb back into his Lexus and drive back him, the route laid by his car's GPS.

I'm fiddling with the radio when "Every Little Thing I Do" by Soul For Real comes on the radio.

"Oh leave it." Jarnel says snapping to the song as he drives. "Back in the day, this was my shit."

I smile seeing this playful side of him as we both sing and dance to the song. I end up going to my iPhone and playing more songs from the 80s and 90s for us reliving our childhood the entire drive back to Boston. I get to snap pictures of us being a two-hour concert in a car.

Sitting in Landon's office in front of his desk I am beaming. "Did Giuliana DePandi just apologize to me on national TV? Wait did she say my name?" I jump up and down.

Landon shushes me. I stop jumping and look at him. He turns off the TV. "This is not good."

"What do you mean?" I ask. "Isn't this what we want?"

Landon paces. "I wanted your name out there, and people to educate themselves on what a transwoman is."

"Hello she corrected herself." I tell her.

Landon sits back on Jenica's couch. "They are going to dig into your past before we have the chance to." He turns his head to me. "They are going to learn about your black family, Jaxson, and your rapes."

My smile changes to horrific shock. I feel like my skin has just been ripped off. Jenica guides me to her makeup chair. She rushes over to get me water. Landon kneels in front of me.

"We need to get out in front of this before they do." He takes the water from Jenica and hands it to me.

I rush through the bathroom into my dressing room and call Jarnel. We talk for about 10 minutes on the phone and end up meeting at Top of the Hub.

Over braised duck and broccolini, I tell Jarnel everything about myself from the time I was born till present including my two rapes and Joseph. He details his life growing up with middle classed black parents in a white neighborhood with his younger sister. Oddly enough meeting me is the most out of the ordinary thing that's happened to him since he was recruited by the Pats right out of college. He also says he never raped that woman that accused him; she was a fan of his that showed up in his hotel room. He rejected her after she got naked in his bed. She claimed rape without a rape kit; it infuriates me that I had TWO done with DNA from my rapist who wasn't accused yet Jarnel was accused with no rape kit and almost sent to prison until he appealed to the girl's mother. His mother talked to her mother and actually brought her to church. The girl's mother ended up getting the truth out of her and sent her to a convent shortly after her dropping the charges. He tells me people still think he paid her off, but he didn't. He asks after we "break up" if we can remain friends; I say yes. He tells me he's in love with a girl who's finally showing interest in him now because we're together. I tell him it's okay and to not feel bad. He asks me if I have someone in mind for when we break up.

"When we do break up, I want to be the one who does my own thing for a bit." I laugh. I want to tell him that I do have feelings for him, real feelings. But I know he doesn't return them. "Dating is exhausting."

He laughs. "With the right person it won't be. No slight to you, but I mean I feel like I made a friend for life."

"And I get say over your next girl." I touch his arm. "No thots." My heart squeezes realizing he'll be with someone else a year from now; and I will be alone.

Our limo pulls up to the red carpet at the Kodak Theatre on a hot July day. Jarnel steps out first and reaches back for me. There on the ESPY Awards 2006 red carpet we go public. The flash of cameras are blinding. LeBron James takes over the E!News mic to ask me.

"Who are you wearing?" He shoves the mic under my face.

Blushing I respond. "Elie Saab" The camera pans my yellow strapless dress with floral embroidery and waist bow. "Shoes by Louboutin." I flourish my gold peep toe pumps.

"And your hair and makeup is flawless, lady." LeBron kisses my cheek. Jarnel fakes jealousy by pushing LeBron away. "Eh eh chill. I won't steal your woman. I mean I probably will because damn. Nah." Jarnel and LeBron play fight. "Beautiful couple. Glad you're both here. Desiré, thank you for your strength and courage. Truly. You're an inspiration." He kisses my hand, and Jarnel slaps him playfully. "Okay okay I deserved that." I hug LeBron before leaving. Jarnel does too.

Inside we sit through all the awards being handed out. He and the boys present Best Coach/Manager. When the New England Patriots tie with the Pittsburgh

Steelers for Outstanding Team the place erupts with cheers. Jarnel hugs me, picks me up, and kisses me. Onstage they all congratulate each other with Tom speaking for everyone.

Then the one category Jarnel is nominated for: Best Male Athlete. He's up against fan fave and ESPY Award host for the evening Lance Armstrong. I grab his hand and kiss it. He smiles at me. When Jarnel's name is called as the winner he continues to clap. Guessing he thinks Lance won I turn to him.

"Babe, they called your name!" I tell him. He looks at my lips reading them.

His face turns from congratulatory to stunned. He slowly stands up, and I wrap my arms around him. He wraps his arms around me and begins to cry. The team rushes him as he moves onstage. Collecting his award in his hand while the screen behind him plays all of his plays leading up to the Super Bowl.

"OH MY GOD I WON!" He exclaims over the standing ovation. "I didn't prepare a speech I'm so sorry." He squints at the camera while I pray he doesn't say something weird. "Okay thank you to the Lord for making this all possible and for guiding me here." Everyone applauds. "Thank you to my mom, dad, and sister. Coach and the boys. My friends back in Wellesley. My trainer Gunner Peterson. But most of all..." he pauses as he looks at me. The crowd goes silent. "Recently I was accused of a very heinous crime. I was proven innocent, and the person admitted she lied. Let me tell you there wasn't alot of discussion between me and you, boo boo. I tried to keep it out your ear. But you never left my side. You never ran away. And I thank you for that. You are my hero. You are my best friend. And you are the love of my life. I don't care who knows either." Tom whistles. "I love you, and thank you for choosing me. I choose you right back. God Bless, everyone." Applause erupts as he winks at me walking backstage.

We make love in the back of the limo leaving the ESPY Awards that night.

Staring at his ceiling the next morning I realize our fake dating has turned into actual dating. We dine at Top of the Hub in Boston, The Ivy in Beverly Hills, and various other restaurants around the world either together as a couple or with his teammates to actual dates sitting at home together, doing a cooking class at The Fairmont Copley, or dinner with my extremely small group of friends. He finally meets the Andersens.

Later that evening Dad is suspicious at dinner. Mom, Alicia, Bryant, Monica, and Rachel question us about our relationship. Suddenly Dad gets up and Jarnel follows him as they disappear to the living room. I don't even budge, then I panic wondering if Jarnel has confessed the details of our relationship (especially the contract). I quickly stand up and rush into the living room to see Dad and Jar chucking it up like old college buddies. I walk over and sit on Jar's lap. He wraps his arms around my waist and because he's so tall is still face-to-face with me. He kisses me.

Out of the corner of my eye I see mom smile in the doorway.

In his bed we snuggle naked under his silk sheets after our last sex session.

He kisses my forehead how he always does. "What if I asked you to marry me?" He says as he pecks my forehead. "Hypothetically speaking."

I did and didn't expect it. "Well hypothetically speaking I would probably say yes." I couldn't believe I said it. Three months of fake dating and two weeks of real dating, and I'm thinking about marrying this man? Was I nuts?

"You know...I've never been with a..." I nod at his response. "But I like you. I can't explain it."

"You mean you like me for my personality and not my genitals? How shocking."

He tickles me till I scream. Then he kisses my temple. "I'm just saying. I don't know you got me feeling some kinda way." He pauses. "Wait remember in the movie theater?" I nod. "When you let me have some of your food."

"So me sharing Sour Patch with you got you loving on me?" I ask. In disbelief

"Damn you making a brother confess his damn feelings like a bitch." He laughs. "Yeah. You look out for me."

I sit up straight, and he follows...worried. "If we are going to be together for real cut it out with that fake ass ghetto accent. And don't tell me that's how you talk cuz it's not. You are educated and have a good job plus I know your dad is a judge, and your mom is a Head Nurse at MGH. You and I know damn well you were raised in Wellesley, MA. And second I'm a transwoman, Jarnel. What happened to loving me for my personality? Where's that guy at right now?" He looks away bashfully. "You cannot keep saying "I love you despite you being a transwoman." There's no despite. Either you love me, Jarnel, or you don't. There's no conditional terms."

He grabs me by the waist, pulls me close, and kisses me. "I love you period end of story. Sometimes I slip back into old habits. I'm sorry." In his normal voice. "See girl, you keep me in check. Nobody talks to me like that. Only you."

"Well someone has to. And I love you too....you big knucklehead." I kiss his nose.

"Knucklehead? Come now." He tickles me before kissing me.

We both take the weekend off and fly to the St. Lucian. We lounge by pool at the Sandals Grande. We make love about ten times that weekend. On the plane home he tells me he chose St. Lucian because he originally was going to take me to Negril, Jamaica but researched me being a famous transwoman I could be shot and killed possibly by police. Jamaica is very homophobic, and there are no laws protecting trans or gay people there. I smile knowing how important I am to him. I lean into that nook again although we're both fully clothed sitting next to each other on a plane. He kisses my forehead with his arms wrapped around me and our feet up in the reclining seats. I can honestly not remember a time in my life I had been this happy.

CHAPTER 26

Talent.

I stand backstage while my other costars are called out. Hunter stands onstage with a mic in front of five hundred fans in the Grand Ballroom of the Fairmont Copley Plaza Hotel.

"This woman needs no introduction, but I'll give her one anyways." He reads from his cue card in front of the cast. "New to our cast last year this woman, excuse me, transwoman." He pauses as the crowd explodes. "This transwoman has changed the face of daytime. My co-star and the sweetest person I know please welcome Desiré Andersen."

As I walk to the front of the stage I get a standing ovation. I shimmy to hug Hunter, and he holds onto me tight. I walk behind him and hold hands with Jenica, and Blaine holds my other hand.

"Without further adieu." Hunter throws his cue card in the air. "Oh hell no. Jillian Collins" He begins bowing as she walks out. Another standing ovation ensues as Jillian walks onstage waving. She pretends to smack Hunter in the head before hugging him. She waves again and squeezes between Blaine and I onstage.

"This is your cast of 2006 of the BET soap '*The Pretty & The Powerful*,' folks." Hunter says while turning around and applauding us. "Oh wait. One more. I have a little surprise for everyone." He turns towards the crowd and pops his collar. "The show has made amazing strides with Desiré's addition, but now it's time…" he takes the mic and walks the length of the stage. "Time to give you what you want and need. What's that mean? Well the return of Molly's first husband Bruce of course." I feel Jillian's hand lock around mine. "Please welcome returning cast member Russell Edwards."

The room erupts onstage and in the crowd with applause. Russell Edwards ascends from the corner of the stage Hunter stands. The tall slightly tan daytime legend walks onstage in a crisp white suit and matching loafers. He flashes a pearly white smile while waving before going down the line shaking the cast's hands. He walks up to Jillian and kisses her on both cheeks. She keeps a lock on my hand before he moves back to waving to the crowd.

"It's gonna be okay." I reassure her. She stares at me blankly.

Landon rushes into the lobby past guests and staff to the elevators; while I pose and take pictures with fans at a table with Hunter. Landon pushes past the elevator doors and runs into the crowd and looks for me; I notice Landon frantically searching for me. He sees me and motions for me to come towards him.

"Hey guys, I will be right back. Give me two seconds." I rush over to Landon as he pulls me backstage.

"You were nominated for Supporting Actress at the Daytime Emmys." He blurts out.

I stand before him speechless. "I got nothing."

"Hello. Hello everyone." Landon says over the mic as I resume my place next to Hunter. Hunter looks at me confused, but I beam. "My name is Landon Hughes. I am Desiré Andersen's manager, but I do work closely with the production staff on the show. They okayed me to come here today and announce some major news. This year at the Daytime Emmys the show 'The Pretty & The Powerful' has received multiple nominations. Outstanding Drama Series, Outstanding Writing and Directing for a Drama Series, Outstanding Makeup, Costume Design, Lighting, and Set Decoration as well as Technical Directing for a Drama Series. Jillian Collins was also nominated as Outstanding Lead Actress in a Drama Series." The crowd explodes. "This will be her eighth nomination and possible fifth win." Jillian waves and puts her hand over her heart. "Blaine Breton for Outstanding Lead Actor in a Drama Series, and this is his second nomination." Everyone applauds; Blaine bows. "Hunter Bentley for Outstanding Supporting Actor in a Drama Series. This is Hunter's first nomination." Everyone claps, and Hunter covers his mouth in shock; I rub his back. "And in her first nomination Desiré Andersen for Outstanding Supporting Actress in a Drama Series. Making history as the first openly transwoman nominated for a Daytime Emmy." The crowd explodes as Hunter hugs me. "I am so proud to be a part of this historic awards show event, this show, and Desiré, your career. Thanks, everyone." Landon is applauded as he descends the stage.

I'm being congratulated by fans along with Hunter when Landon comes over. 'The Pretty & The Powerful''s photographer Jimmie Strain snaps a picture of me, Hunter, and Landon together. I pull Landon aside.

"I think Jarnel is going to propose" I whisper.

"Dee, no." Landon reasons. "You cannot fall in love with him. I understand that somehow along the way your fake relationship became real, but it's only real to you. Honey, he doesn't love you no matter what he says. It's part of the contract ya know? His people haven't reached out to me about extending the agreement. You have to let this go. You two can become best friends like Leonardo DiCaprio and Kate Winslet or George Hamilton and Alana Stewart. So no I won't talk to him for you; I won't hurt you unnecessarily. You don't need that." He hugs my shoulders. "You will find your forever man, trust me." He kisses my forehead before leaving.

I put on a fake smile and continue greeting fans. I decide to not bother telling Landon the details of my relationship with Jarnel. Once we're engaged he'll find out soon enough.

CHAPTER 27

Scandal.

O n the phone with the Hampden County District Attorney I'm told my two statements from my rapes will suffice; I do not need to testify in court. She apologizes for her predecessor's mishandling of the situation. I hang up before we get into a deep conversation.

Jarnel sits on my dressing room couch playing Angry Birds on his phone. I sit next to him, and he stops playing to kiss my cheek.

A noticeably more buff Shayne stands shirtless in his red boxer briefs on the scale in his very masculine bathroom, looks down, and smiles. He flexes his very fit body in the mirror before turning off the bathroom light and hopping under the white flat sheets in his Tempurpedic bed. He stares up at the ceiling. He rolls over on his side and looks at the piece of paper on his desk that has Desiré underlined and my cell phone number on it. He rolls to the other side, turns out that lamp…the only light source in the room at the moment.

Joseph sits nervously shaking his leg until his name is called. He walks into an office. As the door closes it reads "Casting Director."

Jarnel and I are photographed jogging at Castle Island. We're also photographed holding hands as we get ice cream from the Original Boston Frosty ice cream truck; we take a picture with the owners Matt and Danny. I walk a child wearing a "Make-A-Wish' tee on the football field at Gillette Stadium to meet Jarnel. Jarnel and I sit at a table in the middle of Maggiano's with Tom Brady. He starts telling how he wants to win enough Super Bowl rings to fit every one of his fingers. I tell him good luck.

Sheleen is fitting me in the custom made red ball gown complete with mask when Jillian storms in.

"I cannot believe they hired Russell back." Jillian spits. "What the fuck were they thinking? Who'd I piss off?"

"No one." I reassure her. "Listen it's a ratings thing only."

"Let me enlighten you on my history with Russell." Jillian proceeds to tell me how Russell was hired as a foil two years after the show's debut to break her character up from her then co-star whom was a popular pairing; Russell's character was hired by her co-star's ex-wife. Russell's character 'Bruce' ended up falling in love with her character 'Molly' for real as did 'Molly' for 'Bruce.' They enjoyed a successful pairing as did Russell and Jillian off-screen until Russell was rumored to be dating the newest Ingénue. They broke up after it was reported she was pregnant with his child. Immaturely she got him fired, and he was doing off-off-off Broadway as far as she knew.

"Close." Russell eavesdrops walking in fixing his tie in the mirror. "I never slept with Montana, and I was teaching drama at Emerson College here in Boston this entire time. But good to hear you admit you were immature."

"So all these years you held in the truth waiting to pounce?"

Russell laughs. "When the woman you love believes a rumor over you, you tend not to fight to be with her."

Jillian thinks for a second. "I am sorry for how I treated you. I was an ass."

"True. But water under the bridge. I'm here for the work and the fans." He smoothes his hair.

"Well great." Jillian walks away. Russell smirks at himself in the mirror.

When Sheleen's done, I walk to our soundstage. As I walk on-set, Blaine, who's directing again, shows me my mark. He sweats more than usual because this is our first live show.

Blaine takes his director's position as everyone is now in place. "And action." He yells.

I walk up to Molly and Bruce sitting at the table. Molly stumbles when she sees me.

"Um so." Molly tries to explain.

"You tell me not to see Milo, but you sit here cavorting with your husband's older brother?" I spit.

"Well technically she was my wife first." Bruce sarcastically says.

"Whatever. I need a drink." I turn before sitting down. "Waiter, get me-"

The waiter comes over, and it's Joseph. I lose all train of thought and stare at him. What is he doing here?

"What are you doing here?" I think out loud.

"And cut." Blaine shouts. He stomps over. "What is going on?"

"Sorry he's my ex-boyfriend." I say to Blaine still looking at Joseph.

"Oh hell no. Security." Blaine calls.

"No I promise I'm not here to harm you. I just...I want to-" Before Joseph can continue Sharlene stomps over.

"What the hell? This is live." Sharlene scolds me. "Who are you?" She asks Joseph.

"Joseph Pagano." He extends his hand, but Sharlene doesn't shake it.

"We have to now write him in. This was live, folks." Sharlene walks back.

Jillian smiles. "Not so calm with your ex around are you, dear?" She walks by me.

Thankfully Sharlene was quick on her feet, and Joseph's waiter ended up being a guy 'Nina' talked to online. The show ended up having the highest ratings since its debut in 1990.

Now I stare at Joseph as he sits on the couch in my dressing room. He stares back at me, through me. Words escape me at the moment. But he has plenty to say.

"I don't care how crazy I look or desperate." He begins. "I was wrong to walk away from you, from us. And now I am here literally begging for a chance to be back together. If you say no then I will understand, but let it be because you've moved on in your heart and not your pride."

This is not how I expected my day to go. I'm still at a loss for words. "I'm with Jarnel." I couldn't think of anything else. My shock prevents me from seeing my phone with "Jar-Jar calling" lighting up behind me on my makeup table.

Jarnel sits in his brand new silver Mercedes Benz sedan in front of a gas pump. "Hey boo boo. So my mother wants us at their house this weekend. I have a big surprise for you. Plus I'm going crazy downstairs if you know what I mean." He laughs. "Boo boo, six weeks with no nookie makes Jar-Jar a crazy man. Damn training. I wanna win a Super Bowl ring for you. That's gonna be my new goal." He pauses. "I love you so much. See you tonightl Okay bye."

I'm still staring at Joseph in shock. He kneels down in front of me and takes my hand as a tear falls from my eyes.

Jarnel finishes pumping his gas and walks into the convenience store portion of the gas station. As he's walking up two police officers (one Hispanic and one White) stop him. An argument ensues, they try cuffing him, but Jarnel tries to break free. The Hispanic cop hits him in the leg. Jarnel crashes to the ground on his knee shattering it in four places. The White cop sticks a gun to his ribs and shoots him. Both cops stand back and watch a handcuffed Jarnel bleed out in front of the gas station. Patrons inside and out stand around shocked.

"Why are you here?" I demand.

"Because I love you." Joseph admits.

I roll my eyes knowing he's just as sad he lost his shiny new toy. "Oh really." I apply my eye makeup in the mirror while he pulls up a chair and sits next to me.

"I went on all these different dates. I was set up by everyone I know and went online. And every date ended with me feeling no closer to finding what I want. Know why?"

Because I want you. I think to myself. *He's so predictable.*

"Because I want you." He says. "I want to be the one you make love to. The one you wake up next to. The one you go to bed next to. The one you share every intimate little detail with. That's who I want to be. Please let me. Please. I know I fucked up; I do. But I would give up anyone and anything to be with you. No one is more important. No one. Don't you think there's a reason we keep coming into each other's orbit. Since COLLEGE! Come on. Don't you get it? This is the universe saying…"

Fed up with his rambling. "I'm in love with someone else. I love him."

"But you are in love with me too." He correctly states.

I stare at him through my mirror and can't say a word back. He's right; I do love him. It's different from Jarnel, but there it is. My feelings for Joseph and Jarnel are equal parts of my heart. But Jarnel doesn't just say what I want to hear, when I want to hear it; he is present. Joseph and I know what the other is saying before we say it. There's a connection and link there that Jarnel and I will NEVER have. Two sides of the same coin. They both have my heart, and I can't deny it. But why is Joseph here? Oh wait he knows from tabloids and *E!News* that he has competition. And he's afraid after ten years of us being in each other's orbit like he said I will not end up with him. Then the most important question in the world hits me: in love how do you follow your heart when you have a past with someone and building a future with someone else.

We stare at each other in the mirror of my dressing room. Preoccupied with our conversation I ignore my phone vibrating next to me.

CHAPTER 28

Lifestyle.

Jarnel's death is all over the news. *"E!News," "Extra," "Hollywood Insider,"* and every daytime show. Wendy pulls me aside after Joseph and I emerge from my dressing room to tell me. I crumble under the weight of the news. Joseph prevents me from falling. I break down in his arms as he carries me back inside my dressing room.

I ignore every call from his friends and mine even my parents. I just lay on my bed staring into the future Jarnel and I will never have. You never understand the term "heartbroken" until you experience it. I felt like someone had reached into my chest, broke my heart in half like a soft French Baguette, and left it there to sit.

I listen to his voicemail over and over while lying on my bed at my apartment. My face is stained with tears as I have been crying for three hours straight. While he was being murdered I was having sex with a guy who rejected me years before. I'm a selfish bitch, and I deserve every bad thing to happen to me that can. I deserve not to live anymore. To add insult to injury the police gave me his belongings…an engagement ring was in his breast pocket.

My front door opens and closes then Alicia walks in and crawls in bed to cuddle with me. A soft knock raps at my door till Landon walks in.

"Hi, sweetheart." Landon knows I can't talk so he continues. "I know you trust me so we need to take a drive. Go on and get dressed."

He's right I do trust him. I get up, get dressed, and look in the mirror. I no longer look a young 25, but an old 35. I slather Oil of Olay cream on my face, pull my hair back into a messy ponytail, and grab my purse as Landon walks me out. Alicia runs after me and hands me sunglasses. I guess my eyes were worse than I thought.

Inside Landon's car I look out the window in silence. The entire ride to Goodwin Procter is silent.

In the conference room Landon and I walk in to sit across from two stern faced male lawyers but next to Ritchard. Apparently Ritchard worked here back in the day.

"Darling," Ritchard begins. "These are Jarnel's attorneys. Apparently before Jarnel died he changed some things in his will." Ritchard shuffles through papers. "Two weeks ago he came to them and updated you as his beneficiary as he planned on asking you to marry him. And he left you this letter." He hands it to me. "You can read it if you want."

Without saying a word I get up and walk out of the room and go into the hallway tearing open the envelope like a kid on Christmas.

"Dear Dee, Hopefully if you're reading this I am old and grey and we've adopted two kids and have a litter of grandkids. I know I've explained to you when I proposed, but I just wanted to explain again in case you forgot-I choose you. When I told you about that girl I loved I was lying to you. It was you I was talking about. I can't say I've ever hooked up with a dude or a transwoman before, but when my manager told me about you and your story I saw your YouTube clip. Raw passion and powerhouse talent. I thought "this has got to come from somewhere." I want you to know I do love you. I guess at first I didn't think you'd love me that's why I was talking like I was expecting us to end things. I was waiting for you to stop me. I realized you wouldn't so that's why I finally got the nerve to propose. Again I'm sure I have already explained this by the time you read this. But I do love you, boo boo. I know our road was probably not smooth, but I'm just glad we traveled down it together. Anyways this is getting sappy. Don't you dare tell Brady I wrote any of this I love you, boo boo. See you when you get here."

I completely fall into a puddle of tears on the floor. Jarrika and Darnell rush out and try helping me up as does Landon. The strength of three people cannot lift the broken spirit of this transwoman…I'm too heavy for them. Ritchard decides to not struggle to help me up, but sits on the ground with me gently rocking me as another damn of tears breaks through.

As morning breaks I wake up in Jarnel's bed. The image of him rolls over and smiles at me. I smell his cologne in the air. I walk over (fully clothed from yesterday) to his walk in closet and stand engulfed by his scent and presence. My phone is ringing, but I don't answer it. It's Joseph. I listen to the voicemail while lying in Jarnel's bed, but erase it immediately.

In the same outfit at the same table with the same set of individuals I sign to get his temporary brownstone on Newbury Street, his future condo at the W Hotel that's being erected in Boston by 2009 (he already paid for it), his Mercedes sedan and Porsche Cayenne SUV, and $10 million of his $50 million fortune. The remaining $40 million as well as other small personal effects are left to his mother.

I stand in the rain in all black under the umbrella held by Ritchard at Jarnel's grave while his sister, mother, and female cousins sing "Jesus Loves Me." My eyes are dry of tears, but cannot move from his coffin. I feel like as long as I see his coffin lowered into the ground I will be able to make sure he's safe if I know he's in the ground.

His mother breaks down in the choir. I instinctively walk up to her and help her stand next to me. We elected not to have a wake, so she looks up at me.

"Will you please say something to everyone before we let my baby go?" She begs. "He loved you so much and your words will help us all. I know it."

Jarnel's father, who's within earshot, replaces me next to Jarnel's mother. I walk near the coffin and look out at everyone.

"Words cannot express the pain all of us are going through. Senseless act of..." I stop. "The press wants me to speak about this. I will not. Not to them, but to you I say this. It's 2006. These particular police officers said our Jarnel looked like a suspect they had been pursuing. Well it turns out the white cop was connected through friendships to the girl who recanted her rape allegations against Jarnel. In their narrow minds he was a football player who got off with rape. We all know he didn't do it. We all know he wasn't a thug with a gun like they said. They didn't even find a gun on the scene with his prints. Whatever happens to those officers whether they get suspended from their jobs or die miserably is not our concern. God will handle that; hopefully 10 years from now we will not have to deal with such atrocities in our culture. God brought this beautiful individual named Jarnel Rodney Jeffries into our lives; He will deal with the sycophants that took Jarnel away from us." The crowd gives me a couple "Yes Lords" and "Amens" so I press on. "I am done crying over Jarnel's death. That was a moment in a long life. I am going to spend the rest of my days smiling because of his life. How much joy he brought to me and you all. He wasn't a monster; he was a man. He wasn't an enemy; he was a friend." I turn to his coffin. "Thank you for coming into my life. You've changed it forever." I kiss the coffin as it's lowered into the ground. "I love you, boo boo. And I always, always will."

Jarnel's mother, sister, and female cousins once again sing, this time, "I Love The Lord."

Alicia hugs me in the living room as movers take boxes out of my bedroom and through the front door. Ritchard, Kimberly, Bryant, Krissy, Steven, Monica, Rachel, and Crasso gather behind us.

Ritchard interrupts our hug "Okay, you ready to head out, Dee?"

I pull back to look at Alicia. "Are you sure you don't wanna join me? His brownstone has three bedrooms. Everything's fully furnished." I reject Joseph's incoming call.

"When you need a moment of peace and quiet away from the crazy your room will be here. You're only taking your clothing right?" She asks.

"Well and my desktop and laptop, but yes essentially." I hug her. "I'm gonna miss you."

"You're queer. You're a T ride away." She laughs. "Sorry I know queer means something else today, but we've been saying it forever."

"Whatever." I don't feel like educating her right now; I simply laugh.

I blow a kiss as I leave; Ritchard follows me out. The plan is Ritchard will get me settled for a few hours and the rest of the family will come over tomorrow. I just need a few more nights alone.

At Radio City Music Hall in New York City my limo parks idle. The door opens, and I step out on my gold satin Manolo Blahnik pumps. As I stand I push back my now bone straight hair that barely skims my breasts but not is flipped over my shoulder. I let go of my gold sequin strapless Atelier Versace gown; I picked gold in case I win it'll match my Emmy. I walk the red carpet alone. Hunter sees me and comes over to pose for photo ops. E! News is the only press I stop at. Giuliana hugs me before asking me whom I'm wearing. She tells me she's sorry for my loss and hopes tonight's win helps me smile.

As I stand with my eyes closed on the darkened stage, I reflect on how far I've come in my life. The crowd applauds when my name is called.

"Ladies and gentleman." The overhead announcer says. "Please give your warmest of applause to tonight's Outstanding Supporting Actress first-time nominee Desiré Andersen. And last year's winner for Outstanding Younger Actor and nominee tonight please welcome Tom Pelphrey."

The lights go up onstage revealing me. I am so nervous I don't extend my hand to Tom. He does, and I realize my cue. My sweaty palm grips his, and he winks. One of those "Just do like we rehearsed, and you'll be fine" winks.

Looking out at the crowd as we deliver our lines, I catch a glimpse of someone walking up the aisle towards the door; in the sea of people I recognize "that walk." The person's head turns, and I see his eyes. For a split second I forget where I am and that a billion people all over the world are watching me. I quickly recover with my punchline.

"Yeah, but will he make Mr. Blackwell's Best Dressed list?" I ask Tom. "Um I don't think so." The crowd laughs.

Tom fires back. "Whatever." He puts his fingers in the shape of a W.

Moments after announcing Ellen Degeneres the winner of Outstanding Talk Show, I am seated in the front row next to Joseph.

"Please welcome to the stage last year's winner for Outstanding Supporting Actor Greg Rikaart."

As the announcer summons and Greg ascends the stage, I look over at Joseph; I'm completely ignoring Greg and his presence in front of me.

My life hasn't exactly gone how I planned it. I think to myself. *Statistics say as a Black transwoman I should be homeless, working in the sex industry, disowned by my family, no friends to speak on my behalf, beat up, raped, or murdered. Well I guess some of those things are true.* I look at the empty seat Jarnel was supposed to sit in. *But you know I am finally happy.*

"And the winner of the Daytime Emmy Award for Outstanding Supporting Actress is…Gina Tognoni." Greg exclaims.

The crowd erupts. I stand up to give Gina her standing ovation. As she walks by I hug her. I look over at Landon two rows back. He mouths "Next time." I nod.

CHAPTER 29

My life becomes a series of routine behaviors: work, home, appearances, and family. I keep putting off poor Giuliana for an interview. I'll do it one day.

I still reject all of Joseph's calls and send him to voicemail. Unbeknownst to me his father passed away from a heart attack. His mother still runs Pagano's, but Joseph got called by some agent. Now he and Marcus have their own show on The Food Network called "Pizza Brothers" where they receive nominations from different pizzerias around the country and renovate them. This all happened within a matter of weeks. Marcus has been going to school for construction and design. Joseph has his engineering degree from WNEC. Marcus married that waitress from Ruby Tuesday's, Isabel. Landon told me Joseph keeps trying to reach out to me.

With my added wealth I'm able to hire Alicia as my Personal Assistant full-time, and my friend Connie actually becomes my Accountant. I hear through the grapevine Leelee ended up meeting Shayne at a bar, and they moved to West Springfield after they got married. Connie reports to me Leelee dropped all of her friends after their wedding, and only hangs out with Shayne. By chance I end up running into another childhood friend Miguel Rodriguez. The only way to describe Miguel is a heterosexual, serious version of Ricky Martin. Miguel is working security at diVas. I bump into him on one of me and Alicia's trips back home for Thanksgiving. Through a few chats fueled by three Midori Sours, Miguel moves into one of my three guest bedrooms and becomes my Personal Bodyguard. I make a note to myself no more delicious Midori Sours.

As I'm walking around Boston with Miguel nipping at my heels I see Aunt Prissy with her family. I manage to avoid being seen, but walk right into a mob of my fans. The cover of InTouch reads "Still humble mourning the death of her love."

Back at my new brownstone I grab my towel and drink while dressed in a bikini and cut off shorts and walk out the door without locking it. I walk up to the roof and join Alicia who's sprawled out on a lounge chair. I lather up with 50SPF Sunscreen and sit next to her. She pours me a glass of the ice cold pink lemonade she made. I take it, sit down, and sip it as we lay in the sun together.

EPILOGUE

Alicia and I walk back into my new place. She locks the door behind her. I show her around, as my phone rings with "Joseph calling" on my living room coffee table.

We walk into my bedroom, and I tell her when I move into the W Hotel she can take this place, but she feels it's far too fancy for her.

"I just don't think it's right for me." She says. "You really should sell it after you move." She continues without letting me interrupt. "And take the proceeds of the sale of the condo and furniture, keep a few pieces, and give all the proceeds to Make-A-Wish."

I think about what she says and nod. As we turn to leave I catch a glimpse in my closet. That box Dorothea gave me. The doorbell rings.

"I'm sure that's our crazy family." She walks towards the front. "I'll get it."

I walk over to the box in my closet and crouch down to it. I open the lid and slowly move around the journals and photo albums.

AFTERWORD

I just wanted to again give you all a special thank you. I had a goal to write a book that shows a different side of the transworld. The hardship, the struggle, and the ultimate success. This isn't a reflection of EVERY transwoman or transman. It's fiction mixed with my life and a lot of stereotypes. Like me, I wanted this book to defy the odds and be something people remember for years to come. I hope you enjoy it. And reach out to me through social media. Thank you again!

Printed in the United States
By Bookmasters